BRYN SHUTT

www.brynshutt.com

Front cover art by Julia Jacob

Back cover art by Micheline Ryckman

Interior cover art by HSJ Williams

Illustrations by Irina Plachkova, Hannah Rogers, and Kateryna Vitkovska

Edits by Deborah O'Carroll

Proofreading by Cheyenne van Langevelde

PRAISE FOR ILLUMINARE

Set against the backdrop of a vibrant Venice-inspired setting in a world that hints at a wealth of stories to come, *Illuminare* is an enthralling tale that you can sink into and surface still longing for more. With the sharp tang of hope and sorrow mingled on the page and a timeless quality to the prose, this is one fantasy tale you won't want to miss. Bryn Shutt is a truly gifted storyteller. ~Gillian Bronte Adams, award-winning author of OF FIRE AND ASH

Perfect for fans of *Six of Crows*, *The Gilded Wolves*, and *Fawkes*, this story is about a heist, but specifically, the search for hope, a hope that no one can steal away. Poetic and philosophical at heart, this is a luscious read that will have readers hanging for more. ~Cheyenne van Langevelde, author of BETWEEN WORLDS and DILSEACHD-A STOLEN CROWN

An enchanting and immersive read, *Illuminare* dazzles with its wide range of complex characters and tangible setting. In this intricate and poetic heist story, Shutt will keep you guessing as she pulls you along with elements of mystery and touches of romance, and just when you think you've got something figured out, the game will change and you'll realize you, too, are a player trapped in the Masque. ~C. F. E. Black, author of BLADE OF ASH.

Inspired by the majesty of Medici-era Italy, *Illuminare* is a wonderfully poignant blend of fantasy and intrigue. It is both poetic and mischievous in its composition, perfectly complementing Shutt's earlier work, *Dawnsong*. The lyrical prose hints at a full world of adventure yet to come! I am excited for the rest of the series! ~CS Johnson, award-winning fantasy author

You will smile, you will hold your breath—maybe you'll cry a little—and by the end, you'll only want more. *Illuminare* is like an intelligent, clean version of *Game of Thrones* meets *Medici.* And while there are no elves, hobbits, or dwarves, the world within this tale boasts Tolkien level lore. (I swear, it'll envelope you with its sophistication.) In summation, this is a transcendent piece of fantasy fiction that deserves mass devotion! ~Micheline Ryckman, author of THE MAIDEN SHIP trilogy

Shutt's lyrical prose weaves a world both beautifully and painfully familiar. With cutting wit, vivid characters, and historical excellence, her work stands up to the literary greats. ~HSJ Williams, author of MOONSCRIPT

EPIGRAPH

"No one is useless in this world who lightens the burdens of another." — Charles Dickens

DEDICATION

To Chrissy, Sarah, and Micheline—and all who share light through story.

NOTE TO THE READER

Dear amazing reader,

This story both stands on its own and is a prelude to future events. There are some threads that will be unraveled and some left tangled. You have been forewarned.

PROLOGUE

Shadows

Masque, Vawdawr Region

33rd of Sim, 1019 A.R.

Nursery rhymes. They were what was wrong with the world. The shadows had been sure of this for centuries beyond recount. But still, they'd followed the Thief tonight—despite her singing. It was a low, rhythmic sound muffled and at other times harmonized by the gentle dig of oars into rain-pocked water.

But heaven's weeping wasn't the only thing disturbing the surface of the canal.

Streaks of red and gold dye could be seen—and smelled—in the dark water. For this was La Via delle Storie. Theaters lined the right side of the avenue and minstrel halls the left. But down the middle ran the canal and into it, every night, went the used tickets.

The shadows had no idea why dumping dyed paper into a waterway was something that had gone so far down the road of stupidity as to become tradition. But this was the Masque.

People didn't think here, and neither should the shadows. Besides, they were losing the Thief.

She'd pulled her gondola to a stop just under a bridge that flared in a twisting arch over a bend in the canal. Here, the shadows pulled in close, cloaking her.

She didn't appreciate it.

"Chords." The foreign curse came out in a low growl as a slim, black-gloved hand started fumbling in the darkness, groping for—

"Aha!" The sound of metal scraping against mold-slickened stone gave the shadows a shiver and they pulled back as the Thief leaned away and began tethering her little boat to a latch jutting out from the bridge's left wall. Then, before they could decide to pull in again, she was gone, a dark figure jetting over the railings and landing in a soft thud just where the bridge ended and a small walkway began.

The shadows drew up as the Thief stood. The building now before them was like the city, ancient and reeking of secrets, its foundation buttressed by old bones. But what the building held was no secret. On both the back door and the front, in bold letters engraved in the language of Empire, was written: *Kingdom of Albidon, Embassy, established 257 A.R.*

The Thief ignored the door. Instead, she took two steps back and started swinging a small tangle of ropes in her hand like a lasso, then let them fly. The hooks on the end caught on a second story window and, as the ropes slid downward, a small ladder began to materialize. The Thief had her feet in the rungs and was sliding through the open window before the shadows could catch up. Only a few made it in after her.

The room they found themselves in was small, like an afterthought, made of mismatched walls and a sloping roof. Candles burned on both sides of the room, and in the center, on a desk, a single candelabra flickered three yellow lights over a figure slumped in sleep.

The Thief's lips twitched. "Ari." The name slipped from her in a sound too silent to be a whisper, but still, the shadows heard. They looked at the figure again. Golden hair almost red in the warm light, lanky frame, the Albidoni embassy, and that name... The shadows snapped phantom fingers. *Artair d'Argon, the Golden Godsent.*

The shadows knew him. Everyone knew him. They turned back to the Thief. There was something in the way she looked at the sleeping man, the way her eyes had softened as they locked on the bruising under his and the thin hollows of his cheeks. It was as if she cared. Everyone knew the Golden Godsent. But maybe she knew him differently. There was some history there. Now, what was it—

The shadows didn't have time to remember. The Thief was moving again. Toe to heel, she padded silently to a trunk under a narrow, turret-styled window and after testing the lock, flipped open the lid. Clothing, maps, and two pairs of boots more dried mud than leather. She frowned.

"Where's the book?" Her mouth moved with the soundless words as her head whipped around, evergreen eyes scanning the entire room. Books lined the shelves of the back wall, but her eyes kept moving until they landed on the desk again.

If sighs could define frustration, the heave of her chest would have made it into a dictionary. She stood. But instead of approaching the desk, the Thief stepped straight into the shadows. Sliding through the embrace of each one, she moved swiftly then dropped, legs folding, back bent forward.

She made it to the desk and, without raising up from her crouch, slid off a glove, then eased her fingers upwards. She had her hand around a slim volume made of old parchment and too small a cover before the shadows could decide if they were still of any use.

Within less than a dozen heartbeats, she was back out of the room, taking the rope ladder two rungs at a time, followed only by the shadows she'd brought in with her. The others crowded at the window watching her go, their forms lengthened by ever-dimming candlelight.

The shadows knew all the thieves the Masque's gilded halls and murky canals had ever birthed; thieves liked shadows for some reason, sought their blessing like a patron saint. The shadows, however, only cared for the really good ones.

And this woman, she was the best.

She'd been born here, but she was not Vawde, and she had not stayed. No, she was Isadore Rhym: mistress of secrets, queen of mutterers, head of the Albidoni guild of spies and thieves, Lady of Black and White.

What she was doing here now, hundreds of miles from Albidon, stealing from the very embassy that housed her homeland's seat in the imperial city, the shadows had no idea. But they had a feeling they were about to find out.

Instead of heading back to the gondola, Isadore reattached the rope ladder to her belt, then, reaching up, unclasped folded layers from behind her collar and around her legs and let the silken fabric spill down. The newly formed cloak and skirt inked out behind her as she slid her hood up and started down the nearest open-ended alley.

The backstreets of the Masque were just like its canals—narrow, dirty, and wet. Isadore took three of these before circling back into La Via delle Storie and coming to a stop in an arched passageway between two theaters.

Loud orchestral sounds poured from an open side door of the one on her right, while the other building exuded nothingness. She looked about to slide into the silence when the shadows suddenly reared up, one looming over the rest. A man stepped from behind a tower of stacked trunks. A giant of a man.

"Lady Rhym. You have my book?"

Isadore froze. She didn't answer.

The words didn't sound like a threat. But they weren't a question either, not really. The shadows pressed around their Thief as she took a step back, shying away from the lone taper burning on the right-side wall. A single finger went to her lips. Jerking her head towards the left door, with one swift movement, she vanished inside.

"You could have waited," she finally said, feeling over the lintel of a closed door. She hadn't turned around to see if anyone was actually behind her. "Without announcing me to the entire *strada*."

With the twist of a key, the door gave way and Isadore stepped inside. The looming shadow and its owner joined her.

"Forgive me," the man said. He started to press a hand to his heart, then suddenly stopped, and without another word brushed past the Thief and draped himself into the nearest chair with something like a huff or a grunt. “It’s late,” he said. “Or maybe it’s early. Either way, a thing over and done sounds appealing, no?”

Isadore ignored her guest, a happening the shadows were beginning to think was habit. Instead, she struck a match and began bringing the room’s two lanterns to blazing life.

The shadows yawned as the light stretched them out across the floor. Nighttime shadows were nosy, with a penchant for the forbidden, the morbid, and all things that hide in the darkness. But they weren’t keen and sharp like their sun-stark brothers. Give them a wall to drape over or a carpet to lounge on and something to watch, and they could be happy.

Whatever was about to happen here in this dusty antechamber, however, was probably something they’d seen before. Maybe illegal according to some law, somewhere, but not worth repeating...much less remembering. As the second lantern’s light bloomed to full strength, the shadows yawned again.

Wait. A smell. Something sharp, something metallic like copper. Blood. The shadows locked eyes on their Thief’s guest.

He was tall, closer to seven feet than six. They’d observed this already. A black cloak lined with purple silk stretched across his broad shoulders and spilled onto the floor, smothering a few books along with their silhouette companions. He looked to be in the middle of middle age, and despite his rugged build, the man’s face was angular and fine boned...and pale. Too pale.

Hmm. Interesting.

"So, how long have you been with Ink and Quill?" Isadore had seated herself behind the room's only desk. It was a small thing made even smaller by the almost crate-length ledger that took up almost every inch of it.

"A while."

Isadore's eyebrows dipped in irritation. Spies and thieves made their living in what they stole and what they saw. If people said little and did even less, well, it was bad for business.

"Your payment, then? I told you, I want it in lions, not hydras. I want out of this sewer-city." The last line she said under her breath.

"First—" The man shifted in his seat and leaned forward slightly; the movement tightened the wrap of his cloak around his shoulders and the clench of his jaw—as if he was in pain. The smell grew sharper. "Let me see the book."

Isadore shrugged but complied. She held up the volume with its stained pages with the pose of one who had every intention of jerking back should her client decide to make a grab for it.

"Yes." The tall man gave a single nod and with another solitary movement tossed a velvet bag onto the desk. It landed on its side, three glinting gold coins leaking out onto the open ledger. "But it looked better last time I saw it."

"This thing's over six centuries old. I don't imagine it's looked good for a long time. Your name?"

"Kennet Zur."

Oh?

But Isadore just waved her quill in a circle like the name was a fly and she intended to swat it from the room. "I mean your real name, not your guild role. I need it for our records." She glanced up at the man and cracked a rare, coaxing smile. The shadows doubted it was genuine. The weary bend to her shoulders said she'd welcome her bed.

"Kennet Zur."

The shadows, flickered by the light, cast glances at each other.

The Thief growled. The man crossed one long leg over the other and locked both hands against his knee. "My lady," he began. "I don't care if you believe the moon is a loaf of bread and I'm the baker. If you want my name, *that* is my name."

The quill in Isadore's hand took another twirl. The feather might have taken flight if her grip hadn't been so white-knuckled. But finally, with a huff then a shrug, she started writing. Her strokes came out like little stabbing digs into the parchment, but the shadows were barely paying attention.

Their Thief wasn't wrong. The Albidoni guild of libraries and writers had a tradition of titling their current master after the name of Ink and Quill's original founder, a half Albidoni, half Veil chronicler who had died in this very city centuries ago.

...Well, that was one way to look at it. But handed down, passed around from shadow to shadow, was another tale, that of a man who'd died yet lived, slipping through generations and centuries chronicling stories until he had become one himself. But it was a story made like shadows: faceless, fluid, shifting, vanishing for a while, then coming around again. The guild had taken fact and fantasy and made a role out of it. But...

Who knows what the truth really is?

There was one way to find out.

"Well, then." Isadore slid the coins back into their pouch and drew the string. With a twist, she dropped the money into an unseen trunk to her left, then stood. She shut the ledger. "As always, we at Black and White are here to serve, especially our fellow guilders." She held out the book.

The man rose and reached to take it, but Isadore suddenly pulled back, drawing him towards her. Her next words would be real ones. "You know," she began. "I don't like stealing from the count. He's a friend and a friend to Albidon. I only took this job because one guild can't refuse another. I don't know what your politics are, but Artair will be good for our country—"

"Good men tend to be good by default, my lady," the man interrupted. "That I would never deny. But this book was born in war, and war has stolen it again from where it belongs. Not to revolutionaries nor to royals. It belongs to the Library in Prevecost. And it's my job to see that it's returned there. Now, if you will forgive me yet again, I really—"

"Chords!" This time it was the Thief's turn to cut the conversation. "You're bleeding!"

The man threw a glance down at his chest. "Eh? Oh, yes." In reaching for the book, his arm had swept back his cloak, revealing gashed grey velvet stained and streaked with crimson just over his heart. He shrugged the opposite shoulder. "A little run-in earlier. Nothing that can't be mended."

"Are you mad?" The energy in Isadore's words sent her small frame scrambling atop her desk with one hand reaching out to latch onto the tall man's collar. "My lord, there's playing your role, and then there's insanity. You are not actually some storybook immortal and you need a physician. Please."

But the man's only reaction was a sigh. The sound was slow, like time had no hold on when it might end...or when it had begun. Gently, he pried her fingers loose. "I appreciate your concern, but I'd really like to be going now. Still." His hand suddenly tightened around hers for a moment, his lips twitching almost into a smile.

His eyes—they were blue-green, the color of an endless ocean—softened like a father to a child. "Keep caring, little lady, about all the things: your homeland, your friends, those who bring you joy—" His smile stretched into a small chuckle. "Even those who bring frustration. It might bode you well someday. *Addio.*" With that, he swept a bow and was gone.

He didn't vanish, but he moved from the room faster than any man with a stab wound to the heart should—which, by the shadows' recollection, was not at all.

"Follow that man!" The words passed from shadow to shadow through the strada and into a twisting series of alleys and then down. Down beneath the pear tree-lined streets, beneath the canals. Down to where the bones dwelled.

Isadore tried to follow the man. The shadows heard her footsteps, her calls. But she would never find him down here.

The Masque was built on the Masque, except it hadn't always been called that. Once it had been Tu'am, imperial city, master of millions, both in people and in acres. No foe could fight against the Vawdawr Empire and her imperators and hope to win. Except one.

The sea.

With watery claws, centuries ago, she'd come and taken men, miles, and gold to herself, crushing them down deep within her bosom. The capital itself did not wholly fall, but in the floods that had threatened to overwhelm the city, thousands had died, their bodies trapped in sandy graves beneath the ruins.

Eventually, the citizens had rebuilt. Built a city on bones. They called it the Masque. But they knew what they had once been. They would always remember.

Except, maybe some things had been forgotten. As the shadows delved down into the Under, chasing their Thief's client, they knew one thing—they were about to find a dead man. Or...something that had been slipping unseen through Time for far too long.

In the light of three matches, they finally found him. He was leaning against a pillar that had once held up a grand house or maybe even the Senate. It was hard to tell; the shadows had lost some of their bearings in the rush.

But the thing they did notice, the only real thing that was worth noticing, was how the man leaned. Not slumping, panting, or any of the other things he should have been doing heartbeats ago. He had one foot kicked back against the pillar's base while one shoulder rested in a deep groove some forgotten weapon had plunged there. And he was reading.

He had the book he'd taken from the Thief and was methodically flipping page after page. Some he stopped at longer than others, his face flickering from softness to sadness. It was the look of one reading letters from an old friend.

His cloak was thrown back, the bloodstain still streaking down like a badge across his doublet, but no wound could be seen now underneath. *Not normal,* the shadows buzzed. *Not mortal.*

The Immortal Chronicler, Kennet Zur, half the blood of stories, half the blood of stars in his veins, bastard son of a bastard lord. Those were the legends. Those were the tales. And some of them were true. This the shadows could see now. This was the proof.

What does he want?

"Well, well," Kennet finally sighed, dropping the book to his side and letting his other hand twist the matches so their light danced against a mud-caulked fresco. "I think it's time."

Time for what?

"One hundred decades." One light went out.

"Ten centuries." Another match fell silent.

Drawing up into the only light that remained, the shadows held their breath. Whatever time it was, whatever was about to happen, this man had been waiting long—

"One millennium." Everything plunged into darkness.

"Now."

—ever since the day he'd died.

PhantomRin.

ONE

Desmond

Twelve days earlier

Somewhere in the Chantilly Isles

War is the color of three things—mud, blood, and tears. Still, they'd called this the War of the White Poppy. But there was nothing clean or snow white about it, only the Masque's confident pride that the white flag of surrender would soon wave over Voorst. The windmill capital of the Chantilly Isles would fall and their resistance would go up in a blaze of dragon fire. No one questioned the certainty of this eventuality. They only waited for the *when*.

And no one waited more desperately than Desmond Edenry.

"Captain, sir!"

The sound so close by sent Desmond all but jolting in his saddle as he ripped his eyes away from the sunless, smoky dawn. The smoke that rose over the nondescript Chanti town before him was from hearths not destruction.

Its *burgemeester* had heard what the Falcon knights had done to the castles and villages before his. He'd no intention of a repeat. So, at the first sign of blue-and-black banners topping his hillside, the man had thrown open his gates and surrendered.

"Count Artair wants you. He's up there."

Desmond's eyes landed on the speaker standing right next to his leg. *Chords.* He hadn't even noticed the boy approach. The page was breathing hard and sputtering from his run. With one finger, he pointed towards the small walled community and the lone white-stone windmill that towered above it.

"Chords," Desmond muttered, this time aloud. Swinging one leg up and over his horse, he jumped down. The sucking feeling of mud as his boots connected with the soggy earth sent a subconscious shudder down his spine. "Here." He tossed the page his reins. "Take him to St. Clair. Tell him to put him with the others still recovering."

Rounding his mount, Desmond gently ran a hand down the horse's right flank. A gash mostly turned to scar puckered in the skin. Any experienced eye could tell it was a battle wound. A pike maybe, a broadsword? Desmond didn't remember. He just knew when he'd gone down, rolled, and kept on fighting. He barely even remembered which battle it had been. They just flowed one after another like a river with no end.

"Yes, sir," the boy said, head peeking up over the pommel of the saddle. Desmond could hear the sound of his feet in the mud as he eased off his tiptoes and started walking back up the hill towards the Falcons' encampment with the charger. Desmond started in the opposite direction.

Mud meant water. Water was everywhere here. The Chantilly Isles lay scattered across the Salt Sea, the remnants of land that had once been an empire. But the sea had claimed most of that land for itself centuries ago. What remained bobbing on the salty surface was a mad mix of clay, peat, sand, and mud, always mud. The local inhabitants might have found it perfect for growing tulips. Desmond Edenry, Captain of the Albidoni Falcons, just found it wet.

The soggy ground beneath him gave way to rocky sand, then a stream. Scouts had reported its existence upon their arrival here at midnight. The plan had been to attack at dawn, but the burgemeester had just surrendered without a fight. Artair had been happy. All the men had been happy. The fewer dead Chanti there were meant even less dead in their own ranks.

But rarely was such luck on their side. The sun had risen further now, still hidden behind clouds that promised rain. "More wet," Desmond sighed to no one but the muck.

Still, a few paces in, he found himself stooping to one knee and cupping the icy water in his hand. As he splashed it onto his face, his fingers met at least two days' worth of beard. He needed to shave. He needed—

There was a sound behind him, a trickling, sloshing sound, too loud to be from a bucket.

Turning, one hand automatically going to his nearest dagger, Desmond found his eyes landing on a waterfall not a dozen feet away. *Not something to stab, Edenry.* It wasn't large or spilling from any great height. Elms, three of them, crowned its top. He frowned.

The sound the water made as it merged with the stream was peaceful, lyrical. Eldritch. As his hand slid from the dagger hilt, dropping unconsciously into the water, he tried to turn away. The sound was so familiar and yet utterly foreign—not the screams of the wounded, the moans of the dying, the rage of the defeated. Or even the sound of a backcountry mayor now swearing fealty to an imperator leagues away.

He had only avoided hearing this particular one's surrender by slipping away to ride out the area, to see how long the surrounding countryside could sustain two hundred armored knights plus foot soldiers. Artair's page had found him anyway.

The feeling of icy water numbing his skin broke the spell of the moment, and Desmond jerked his hand from the stream with a splash. But he still couldn't pull away. He needed to. He had to. He'd ruin it.

Once, he had been that sound. Once, it had been familiar. Innocent, untainted, a young knight with dreams of defending the helpless and bringing down the darkness. But now? The years and orders had taken his will, warping and molding him into just a sword, an arm of Death fighting another man's war. No water could erase the blood seeping through his skin, down into his bones, tangling itself deep within his soul. Maybe that's why he hated it so much.

"Chords." He heaved himself up. *Thinking changes nothing.*

"You there! Falcon!"

Desmond didn't jump this time as his feet cleared the stream and his hand didn't reach for a weapon. Just a growl, deep and low, reverberated in this throat. There was a special, nerve-rankling tone that belonged to only one class of people, and the voice calling to him now, mere paces away, had it.

Royals.

Turning from the sunrise, Desmond let his gaze drag like cat claws over the figure approaching the stream from the south.

The man sat astride a piebald pony, the sturdy sort bred for long-distance plodding. He rode the bandy-legged beast like a king—not that he was one. Albidon had gotten rid of the pox that had been their monarchy decades ago. But some of the last king's descendants lingered on here and there like the aftereffects of a bad meal.

"I need to know where the Third Army's encamped!" the man called out again, cupping his hands to shout even though he was hardly two body lengths away now. "Have you seen about, oh—" Leather-clad arms rose into the air and started gesticulating wildly. "About a thousand men in grey and scarlet? Preferably still walking upright?"

Desmond drew his sword, and with one downward plunge, let its tip sink into the soft earth. He leaned against the hilt. The voice was royal in every facet, but those movements—Desmond had seen them before. "Laudilas de Glas," he said. The growl in his throat eased into a chuckle as his lips twisted upwards, tugging against the stiffness of his beard.

The man on the horse bent forward, sharp eyes peering over an even sharper nose. "Edenry? Desmond Edenry! Chords."

Laudilas de Glas, prince by blood but actor by need of putting food on things like tables, flipped back his hood, letting loose a wild mane of almost waist-length hair. "I haven't seen you since men were sane. What are you doing out here?" He drew his pony to a stop at the edge of the stream.

It had been another lifetime ago, but Desmond still remembered it. A theater in Maudi Lane back home in Prevecost. People gathered around a stage, laughing, crying, cheering the hero, booing the villain. Forgetting fact to become lost in fiction.

It hadn't been the first show Desmond had seen the could-be prince lead, but it had been the first time he'd been willing to admit that maybe this particular de Glas had found what he wanted on the stage and not in seeking out a throne that people like Desmond were set on believing no longer existed. The older de Glas brother on the other hand—

"So, my brother and his men, any idea where to find them? Because"—Laudilas rose up in his saddle—"I don't think all this Falcon blue is his taste, unless I've gone colorblind." He settled back down with a creaking plop. "Drat that villager, he must have been trying to get me lost." He reached into his vest and pulled out a flask. After fumbling with its cap for a few heartbeats, he took a long draught, then held it out to Desmond.

Desmond shook his head. "Last I heard, the Third Army was west." He eased his sword from the ground and pointed opposite of where the sun was still fighting the heavy clouds for dominance of the sky. "Probably by Breda."

The name brought no flicker of recognition to Laudilas' eyes. Desmond might as well have told him a thousand men had marched off to the dark side of the moon.

"Oh well, west it is," Laudilas finally said anyway, flipping his hood back up. He threw a glance over his shoulder to the town. "Looks like an easy victory here, eh? Lucky." His smiling face had slanted down now into a tight, grim expression. Desmond could only imagine what the young man had seen in the past few years. Not the cheering, adoring faces of a theater audience, that was for sure.

When Albidon had received word that their Accords with the Masque were expected to be honored by sending their armies south, men from all walks of life had found themselves uprooted and shoved into places they would never have intended. Desmond wasn't the only one.

"Oh well." Laudilas bent his waist in a bow, his movement displaying dramatics his expression did not share. Then pulling on the reins, the young man turned his mount toward the west. "Until we meet again," he called, not looking back.

Desmond didn't answer, but he watched until both pony and its owner's scarlet cloak were a mere beribboned speck on the cloudy horizon.

Until we meet again. Desmond remembered a time when he'd have given anything to see any last vestiges of his people's royal family gone for good. But now? A shiver gnawed its way down his spine. He missed the old familiarity of homeland rivalries.

Still— He let his sword fall back into its sheath with a click. "If that boy can't find an army, I doubt he'll have any better luck with the crown even if he used both hands to look." He was muttering to the water again. Chords, he was losing it.

But for a brief flicker of a heartbeat, the questioning thought of what would happen if one of the de Glas brothers actually *was* king crossed his mind. Would he be here, fighting another man's war? Maybe. Maybe not.

Thinking changes nothing.

Unlike the stream, the town was quiet as Desmond passed through its gates, like an artist's illustration that had forgotten the characters. Shops had been shuttered closed and the market stalls stood empty, but unseen eyes were following him from all angles.

The mood was cautious, but curiosity spiced the silence in an undercurrent. Desmond could feel it. These people were not quite as afraid as they could have been. They were lucky they had a wise burgemeester, and it was even more in their favor that it was the Falcons at their door.

The Falcons had two reputations. First, they always won a battle. No matter who had to die on either side, they won. But that's when it ended. There was no aftermath when the Falcons took a place. And if one of them started to feed his baser desires of greed or lust—well, there was another sort of aftermath and another body on the pile.

The windmill tower itself sat in the center of the town, made up of stone on the outside and stairs on the inside, the narrow kind that twisted through the edifice like a mangled spine. Desmond took them two at a time.

It had been three years since he'd been home. Maybe four. He had left Albidon just another knight in the ranks. But seventeen battles and twelve months later, he had found himself captain. Eight months ago, he'd been due for leave. Technically, overdue. But any furlough had been impossible as the Siege of Esendaal had dragged on. But now, with today's victory, minor though it was, he just might score an escape.

He had a list in his head of all he would do when his feet finally landed back home on Preve Dock. Kiss solid, non-muddy ground for starters, then run out of the city and into an open field and shout to the heavens that he couldn't see any water.

He could hear Artair's voice somewhere high in the tower harmonized by another's. The other voice sounded familiar...

The energy of the thought doubled Desmond's steps, driving him—straight into the burgemeester.

This close to the man, Desmond could see he was slight and balding with a face whose lines had once been made by smiles. Today, worry and sorrow were etching into him like a chisel to marble.

"I'm sorry."

But the man only nodded and kept walking by.

I'm sorry, Desmond wanted to repeat, catch the man and fall to his knees. *I'm sorry there's an imperator in the Masque who thinks your land is his just because it was a millennium ago. I'm sorry my people have an obligation to answer that monster's every beck and call. I'm sorry.*

But the man was gone.

Desmond started to climb again. *What are words in the end?* The jadedness inside him curled through his mind like a worm. *Just like water, ever flowing but altering nothing. Just like thinking.*

"You have a list?"

"Of course, I do! And there's this landgrave's daughter in Varr who—"

The conspiratorial words floated out to Desmond as he cleared the last step from behind a closed oaken door. Artair only talked about other men's daughters when he was planning something that was the opposite of escape in Desmond's book.

"Ari." He threw open the door, his tone coming out more like a growl than a greeting. "Who's your guest?"

"Ah, Edenry." A man with a frame comparable to a beanpole unfolded himself from a window seat and flashed a smile made of teeth. "Look who's brought the mail."

Desmond's eyes took in the small, circular room until they confirmed what his ears had heard earlier. The voice did indeed belong to Reginald Hinds: privateer, scoundrel, and most importantly, owner of a ship that took people over water to places that didn't threaten to drown themselves and their inhabitants on an almost daily basis.

"I don't care about letters *from* home," Desmond said, crossing the room and settling himself into the seat Artair had just vacated. "I want to *go* home." He inched two walking fingers across empty space to accentuate his point. "I have leave. So, if you don't have a ship and a departure time, I'm not interested."

"Well, I have a ship." Hinds tapped a finger against a nose startlingly crooked in an otherwise refined face. "But I don't think you're going to like where it's going."

"And that is?"

"The Masque, my boy, seat of the Drakes, home of the Mother, the imperial city reborn—" Hinds' tone might have convinced even a slave to march willingly to his doom.

But Desmond cut him off with a wave of his hand. "No, thanks. I have a religion that keeps me out of hell."

"Pfft." Artair stepped into the center of the room and the conversation. "The Masque's too wet to be hell."

"Ah, but that's the trick," Desmond countered, crossing his arms, the buckles of his vambraces scraping against his breastplate. "Smoke and mirrors."

Hinds shook his head. "You're both ridiculous." Then without any of his former fanfare, he tossed the top package in the stack Desmond's direction.

"Chords, man!" Desmond untangled himself as he lunged forward. The package brushed through his fingers and dropped to the ground with a cascade of noise.

"I assume it's supposed to make sounds that are not *that*? It was delivered to my care in that condition." Hinds held up his hands as Desmond snatched up the parcel and threw him a look made of swear words. The privateer's palms were so flat out that not even a lawyer could have stuffed any blame there. "Take it up with the two ships and however many riders before that who handled it. What's a knight want with music, anyway?"

Desmond didn't answer. A few cuts of twine and paper revealed a splintered cherry wood box. Slowly, Desmond lifted the lid as he sat back down. Against pine-green velvet, a violin lay inside like a body in repose—a body that had been smashed and fractured to pieces.

Desmond felt his eyes squeeze shut, the constant ache in his heart suddenly pressing even tighter. He had learned the violin years ago. To his old master, the process had been a mere training exercise, but for Desmond, it had become something else. A connection to what his people were: lovers of expression, freedom, stories, all that man was and could be.

He'd never been the boy possessed with the wild notion of running off to spend his days as a wandering minstrel telling stories of heroes. He had wanted to *be* the hero. But his music had remained as a reminder that a life lived could become a story told. It was the fuel to the fire that had beat his heart and passion for so many years.

He let the lid fall shut. He didn't want his story told. Not now. If fate had decreed that he live fighting other men's wars, shattering his plans, then this was the perfect tangible representation of that doom.

"You should get off your ship more when you're home, Hinds." Artair's voice cut into his thoughts and emotion, tugging him back into the present. "Remember what your people are really like. You know we'd sooner be dancing and fiddling than fighting. Now, Des, how about a woman?"

That last line yanked Desmond firmly back into the here and now, with a looming threat of the future clearly in its implication. "A what?"

"Oh, you know. A maiden fair." The count's long-fingered hands whipped an hourglass shape into the empty air. His angular face was radiating whatever schemes were inside his head and just about to come out his mouth.

Desmond let his eyes roll—not that the movement could stop this conversation once it had begun. "I'm familiar with the female gender. I think you've been away from your wife too long."

Artair was many things to many people. To the crowds at home, he was tomorrow's glory. To the songsters, he was the Golden Godsent. To Desmond, he was the mastermind of every personal disaster he'd ever known—he was also his best friend.

A hopeless romantic, Artair had eloped at just eighteen with his childhood sweetheart, scandalizing all of Albidon, including his intended, Isadore Rhym. But the people had quickly come to love the count's wildness. It made for a good story. Almost a decade later, and Artair was still just as madly in love. Mentioning his wedded bliss was the perfect diversion. Usually.

"Come on, don't you think marriage will make you happy, Des?"

Chords in flats and sharps. They were really talking about this. *Again.*

"No, I'm quite happy as I am." Well, that wasn't entirely true. Being near too much water was beginning to crack his sanity. But otherwise— "Really. Just fine."

"Well!" Artair stepped closer, a slice of brief sunlight from the opposite window glinting off the gold banding inset in his armor. "Good, because marriage never made anyone happy who wasn't already."

The Imperator favored hanging, then drawing, and finally quartering traitors. After witnessing three such slow, torturous deaths, Desmond couldn't imagine a more terrible way to die, but this conversation was always borderline close.

With a snapping click of his teeth, Desmond stuffed his violin, still cradled in its casket, to one side and leaned forward, bracing his hands on the lip of the window seat. This small-town mayor had denied him a fight, and for that he still had enough humanity to be thankful, but Artair was a different story.

"Hey, Edenry, this looks important." Oblivious to the scrap brewing inches from his crooked nose, Hinds suddenly stepped in front of Artair, blocking Desmond's view of his target. In his right hand was a letter. A large, black seal with equally black ribbons dripped over the front of the missive. Someone had died. The privateer held it out without a word. So, someone Desmond knew, then.

He stood, taking the letter and cracking the seal with one flip of his thumb. He had parents. But they were the frustrating sort one only felt sorry about when they were actually nearby, not forever in a grave. And the only friends a soldier really had were his fellow comrades, and they were all right there. The news couldn't be that bad...

Thorne Holdings, Ltd.
The Masque, Vawdawr Region
Sir Desmond,
It is with great regret that we must inform you of the passing of your uncle Gilbert Thorne on the 23rd of last month.
As your uncle passed from this world without known heirs, the entirety of his estate has been willed to you. As you may be aware, your uncle's holdings included property both in Prevecost and here in the Masque...

Desmond felt his vision blur.

"You all right?"

With one hand, he waved off Artair's worried words, and with the other, he let the letter drop to the floor. Five ragged steps took him to the tower's other window. He was going to be sick. Water rose to greet his spinning vision like a wave from a despised neighbor.

Oh, no, his mind moaned. *Merciful Lord, no.*

"Des!" Artair had picked up the letter, his voice sounding distant and yet way too close. "I had no idea the Building Baron was your kin! Chords, the things you don't say. Do you have *any* concept of how much...?"

The only concept Desmond had as the letter's words flooded through his every sense, drowning out everything else, was that now he was a great inheritor. Now, he had holdings. Now, he was rich, and rich men were many things. But they were never heroes. They graced songs and tales as the villains. If life was denying him the chance to be good, was it trying to make him bad?

Suddenly, granite-hard rebellion rose up inside him like a dyke desperate to cut off the rising water. His breath came fast, his chest pressing against the armor that had once felt like a blessing and now was his bondage.

And gold? Gold would be both the coffin of his hopes and the nails that sealed it shut.

"This changes your marriage prospects *considerably*!"

It changed *everything—*

"The letter's from the Masque." Hind's voice added to the rising maelstrom. "He must have passed away there. Guess you'll be taking me up on that passage after all."

Chords in flats and sharps in every key.

Kennet

Masque, Vawdawr Region
34th of Sim, 1019 A.R.
Thirteen days later

It was hard returning to the city where you'd once died; insulting really, the way the stones looked at you, remembering the taste of your blood seeping into their cracks. But today, Kennet Zur wasn't looking at the sandy stonework that made up the Masque's southend market district. He was looking for a rose bush.

Dawn had finally pushed away the rain of the previous night, leaving the morning air muggy and pungent with the scent of wet pear blossoms. Not even grilling lamb drizzled heavy with fresh olive oil could quite drown out the musky, moldy smell.

"Feta and lamb on a skewer, only four whelps! Come get yours! You there, tall sir, come have a feast with—"

Kennet waved the old woman off with a flick of a coin. He could hear her gasp as he pushed past the food stall. He hoped it was a hydra and not some foreign or forgotten currency that everyone else had abandoned generations ago but was still haunting the edges of his pouch. It was a tempting offer, though... The sudden, sweeping aroma of baking pita almost stopped his long legs. Just because he couldn't die from hunger didn't mean he enjoyed being hungry.

He waved his hand again. This time at himself. *Later, later.*

He found his rose bush ten paces down. The former bush-now-arbor crept up and over a stone wall, then plunged down in long, lazy tendrils that fluttered over empty air like a curtain. Kennet reached out and swept them aside. The scrape of thorns against the stone let out a grating sound, like a quiet but insistent alarm.

"Buying or selling?" The voice came from somewhere in the darkness that met him.

The cuts the thorns had peeled into his hands vanished before he was two steps into the gloom. He usually healed quickly, almost instantly in most cases. But last night's wound had been from a poisoned blade. His body had been too busy kicking the al'am out of his bloodstream to worry about the bit leaking down his clothes.

He'd found it was easy to burn through things like clothing and money. Even his aliases hadn't been immune over the centuries. He'd given up on them, really. He had a name. Let people believe what they wanted when he used it.

"Selling," he called back to the shadows.

The response was a whirling, creaking sound and suddenly the darkness was replaced by a burst of warm morning light. A boy sporting the beginnings of his first beard hopped down from a barrel crowned high with a heavy black curtain and blocked the way.

"Well, let's see it."

"How about I see Piero Givanno, instead?" Kennet sidestepped the boy, sizing him up. "Your father, I'd assume?"

Besides the ability to use his heart as a stopping place for swinging poisoned blades and irritate nothing more than a spymistress, Kennet had found immortality to his liking over the years—except—

Disorientation. It struck him now in a sharp wave. It hadn't been like this at first, but as babes became old men to bury and dynasties rose and fell, it had gotten harder. Harder to remember that time changed things, people moved on. And bushes became arbors.

"Grandfather, actually, and he's not up yet. But—" Kennet felt dark eyes considering him. "You're a chronicler from Albidon, yeah? From the guilds? Papa said you might come someday. Down here." The boy beckoned at Kennet, but the immortal knew the way. Sharp turn right and down three steps.

"The roses. Weren't they a bush?" he called after the boy, following him.

The room they entered was narrow but long, the only light coming from a large pane of glass in the ceiling. Frescoes paneled the walls, but their faces were mostly hidden by shelf after shelf of items. Old ones, new ones, all with stories.

"Pffft, about fifty years ago it was," the boy called back over his shoulder. "A good marker to bring the right people in back then. Now it's a good deterrent to keep the wrong ones out. So, what are you selling today?" He'd rounded a long table and was standing behind it now, hands spread on the surface like a man ready to bargain. "Any Pattzi after you? We won't sell a thing if the guard is looking for it already. Did you nick it from a noble?"

"It did come from a nobleman, yes." Kennet trailed a long finger down an old brass candlestick, a solitary witness to who knew how many lives. "But not Vawde. Albidoni."

"Sinners." The boy spat so hard his shoulders jerked. "I don't care about them. All their posh and class. They used to be slaves. Our slaves. It was a good look for them."

If this grandson of Piero Givanno had possessed any sense—which his mouth was already betraying he didn't—he might have noticed Kennet's hand had pulled away from the candlestick and was drawing into a fist. The silent strain of skin over white knuckles spoke of a dark history. One everyone knew intellectually, and one the immortal knew intimately.

Kennet's mother had been an Albidoni, a slave general. But he didn't think about her. Not even on good days. And today's verdict was still up in the air.

"How much you want for it?"

With a hard breath, Kennet let his fingers unflex and held up his hand. "Nothing. Not money. You will follow my instructions."

"What?"

"Tell your grandfather, *Time and Timeless met; they did not dance for man.* He'll understand. Now listen. Two hours from now, a man from the household of Luca Drake, fourth prince imperial, will come to buy this." He drew out the book he'd taken from Isadore Rhym mere hours before. "Sell it to him. Only him."

"For how much?"

"Oh." Kennet paused at this and shrugged one broad shoulder. "That depends on how His Highness is feeling. Hopefully for your coffer's sake he's in a wasteful mood." With that, he set the book on the counter. He held it there for a moment without letting go, like a parent unwilling to part with a child, even into the care of a doting grandparent.

"That candlestick?" he finally said, pulling his fingers away while jerking his head back to where he'd been standing earlier. "Where did it come from?"

"Oh, that? Hmm, the Bianchis, I think. Rival family's heir took out their heir with it one night in a brawl. Matriarch didn't want to look at the murder weapon, so ordered a servant to toss it in the canal. Servant tossed it here for a few hydra, instead."

City of Bones. That's what they called the Masque. They'd called it other things when Kennet had been a boy a thousand years ago. But ever since the First Empire had fallen, leaving only its capital remaining, the surviving families had been fighting, cheating, and killing their way through the centuries, trying to regain what they had once been.

Idiots that they were, they thought adding more bones to the pile would help. House Drake had been the winners, knifing their way to the top. They'd taken the name of imperator to themselves and now they were building an empire again.

This one was being built on bones, too. Foreigners' skulls and skeletons. But the other families in the city were still fighting. Only one thing bound the Vawde together—

"Whoever's coming for this had better hurry. You know how the streets get on La Notte." There was a shift to excitement in the youth's voice now as he spoke. Festivals, holidays. Even though Kennet had been through thousands of them in every corner of the world, he wasn't numb enough yet to not feel that spark still himself on most high days. But not for this holiday. Not the one that came tonight.

"Yes," he said anyway, turning and passing back by the candlestick, "I'll be sure to pass that along. Well, *grazie e arrivederci*." His arm started to raise in a backhanded goodbye.

"God is dead," the boy called after him. "May the Mother have mercy."

Kennet didn't break his stride. He kept moving. But his hand dropped, locking into another fist. This one was accompanied by an audible crack of knuckles. The phrase the boy had spoken was common enough in the Masque, particularly today. It was like a blessing.

It was a curse. The very reason why Kennet had paid one hundred gold lions for a book that was really only worth sentimentality and why he—

Later, later.

Without a word, the immortal swept from the room and past the rose-petaled curtain and back out into the streets. It was true enough, though. His business transaction had lasted less than half a turn of an hourglass, but traffic had upticked sharply. He'd tried to ignore it before, but now it was impossible to miss—

Red. The color was everywhere. Ribbons, streamers, masks hooked on carts ready for the selling. As he left the southend district, heading up into the higher rings of the city, he passed a statue. Pale marble with the carved figure and face of a woman. Kennet watched as two young girls, both barely beyond childhood, draped the statue in a silk the bold color of new blood.

La Notte della Dama Rosa. The Night of the Red Lady. It was coming. Tonight.

Flicking his cloak back in a wind created with the sweep of his own hands, Kennet turned from the statue and moved on. He stopped at a small cart parked off the Grand Canal and made a purchase. But three chocolate-dipped cannolis later and the only thing the immortal had managed to soothe was his stomach. His nerves still felt strung out.

He'd been like this since last night. His calling was to chronicle stories, not to meddle in their flow. But something was growing in the Masque, something that had sprung up from the rot and death of the First Empire's fall.

It had started slowly, like a mold spot a scrub brush had missed. But it had grown, and now it leeched life from every corner of the city, crowning the highest places. Black like rot, pale as corpses. Red, the color of lies.

The Religion of the Red Lady. Mother Death.

It was what bound the Vawde together, linked like chained slaves. It had to be stopped. But—

"Pass?"

Kennet blinked. He'd been walking too fast or too long and hadn't noticed the guard mere inches from his face or what spread out beyond the man.

There were few things in the world Kennet could look at after one thousand years and still feel like he had as a boy. But one was the Palace Imperial. It sat before him now as it had for centuries, untouched by man or sea, buttressed by five hills behind and the sprawling face of the city to its front. But it had changed masters.

As Kennet flashed his bronze identification tag to the guard and started passing through the palace gates, the feeling of stepping, not into a dragon's lair, but straight into its fang-riddled mouth trickled down his spine.

House Drake had been merchants when Kennet had been young. They had sailed the Salt Sea between Vawdawr and Atherland, building a kingdom of trade. Now, they were building that kingdom again. But this time they intended to take not just the goods of Atherland, but its miles and men as well. Subjugating the Chanti nation that lay between the Drakes and their prize was just a stepping stone.

Kennet paused at a small pool brimming full from the previous night's rain and drew in a slow breath. He wondered for a moment what might happen if he didn't let it out. If somehow his immortality could reach out and hold Time still for just a little while. Pause the wars, the bloodshed, the bondage, the death...

A bell rang out almost overhead. "Bah." Kennet spat out the word along with the air he'd never fully drawn in. Delusions were for the young. Besides, he had a job and he was late for it.

For the past three months, Kennet had been working under contract to the youngest of the Imperator's sons. Luca was nineteen, the junior in a set of twins that had come into the world as midnight had welcomed the new millennium. The Imperator might have gained twins that day, but there was nothing equal about the two children. The eldest, a girl, was powerful, a mind molder, a gift rare and feared.

Luca, on the other hand, was crippled. Sickly since birth, the prince had built his court out of knowledge, books, and mathematics. He might have won himself the accolade of the youngest professor to ever hold a seat at the university. But five years ago, his health had crashed to dangerous lows, leaving the young prince to fight for his life with the same tenacity his father fought for land.

Over the past year or so, the illness had retreated to a stalemate, but its victim still remained confined to a bed or chair. Generally, the public perception of the prince was that of a tame, docile boy who spent his days being read to.

Fortunately for Kennet, Luca was and did none of those things.

So, it was with a loud inward swing of both doors that Kennet announced himself that morning.

"Your Highness?" The greeting trailed off into a question. The room that met Kennet was dark. Heavy damask drapes shuttered the windows. *Odd.* Luca was usually up and busy before Kennet arrived—which, granted, was often late. The immortal didn't *need* to sleep, he just liked to. Sometimes too much.

Feeling his way into the room, Kennet fumbled for a curtain rod. With a heave, he drew back the nearest set of hangings. The room that blossomed into view was a curious one. Its shape was like a hexagon with bookshelves each over ten feet high lining the walls in a geometric weave. But at the head of the room, both enormous and somehow still dwarfed by the bookshelves, was a canopy. Kennet made for it.

At the sound of his footsteps, a figure rose up from the pillows that crowned the bed beneath the canopy. It had the pose and energy of a viper with a grudge. "Dragonspit," it swore.

"Ah, good, you're up. There's a book you need to buy."

The figure's dark eyes framed by even darker brows met Kennet's in a glare. If looks could kill, even immortality might have been in danger. Finally, with a grunt, the prince pushed himself up against the weight of his all but useless legs.

"I thought the reason for your existence in my employ," he finally said with a heavy sigh as his arms folded into a cross over his chest, "was to catalogue the books I already own, not to encourage me to buy more."

"Ah, but what is life without a little encouragement?" The night and subsequent morning had left Kennet in a rattled mood. Words were coming out of his mouth before they ever touched his brain.

"Peaceful."

"You're a Drake, Imperial Highness. What do you want with peace?"

Luca snorted as a spark glinted in his eyes. "Because I'm a Drake, I should hoard things, no? Like a dragon? Well, I choose peace. What do you want? Make it quick. I feel like the underscrapings of hell."

In the dim light that had crept from the front of the room to the back, Kennet could see Luca's face was tight with more than irritation. Pain feathered the muscle in his jaw and exhaustion shadowed under the young man's eyes.

Fall and ruin. Kennet's plan depended on Luca *not* having taken a bad turn and being his usually overly curious self.

His legs buckled him into the nearest chair. Squeezing his eyes shut, he shook his head. People might have assumed that a man sent back from death to chronicle history until its end would take life heartbeat by heartbeat. But that wasn't the case.

Sometimes Kennet moved slowly, barely perceptible to those around him, and sometimes everything within him pounded like the racing hooves of a horse driven by a furious whip. The last few days he had been both of those things.

"Forget it, forget it," he sighed. He shook his head again before opening his eyes, frustration continuing to rumble through his mind.

But as his gaze reconnected with Luca's, he saw a hint of interest slipping through the wall of pain. The two locked gazes for a moment longer until Luca broke away and waved a hand, insinuating the immortal should stay where he was. Then with a flinch, a miss, and another try, he started to tug at a bell pull. Kennet watched him.

If he could stand, Luca Drake, fourth prince imperial, would have towered over six feet tall. But somehow the prince's lanky frame had always struck Kennet as being at odds with his face. It was pale, but not just from sickness. There was a fairness to Luca's skin that spoke of distant Athlander heritage. Its tone contrasted starkly with the darkness of his hair and heavily fringed eyes.

A woman might have found the young man handsome in a beautiful, impish sort of way. But women in the Masque valued power and strength. No one assumed Luca had any of those things. They probably never would.

"So, why this book?" Luca finally asked, letting the rope go and resting his head back against the carved headboard of his bed. His eyebrows had arched into question marks, imperative ones.

Excellent. Kennet mentally rubbed his hands together. *Plan's back on.* He opened his mouth, then closed it. Then puffed out a breath made of nonsensical sounds. "It's a diary, the diary of Adile, the first queen of Albidon."

Luca's brows knotted tighter. "And?"

"That's it." Kennet spread out his hands with a shrug and a smile. "A centuries' old book filled with lady things."

Luca's face twitched. "And what am I supposed to do with this book of—"

"Lady things."

"Yes, that."

Kennet stood. "Oh well, you could read it. Say you own it."

"I own a five-thousand-year-old scroll recounting the Fall itself. I don't think anyone's going to be impressed by a five-hundred-year-old book of feminine musings."

"Lady things," Kennet interjected.

Luca let out a sigh edged with an undercurrent of muttering. "Don't you think the Albidoni are going to want it for themselves? Isn't it probably some sort of national treasure?"

It is *and that's exactly what I'm counting on. But I need* you *as the middleman. Cooperate with me, princeling.*

"You're up to something."

At Luca's sudden, sharp words, Kennet stopped his pacing and spun on his heel. He didn't think the prince had a clue what—who—he really was. Luca was clever, a bona fide genius, really. Kennet hadn't come across very many who truly fit that definition, but Luca did. Still, there was an inkling of knowing in the prince's eyes. He guessed something was up.

"Fine," Luca cut into Kennet's thoughts. "Whatever you're up to, you and that crazy country of yours. I'll play along. How much?"

"What do you think?"

"You're the professional archivist."

Kennet ran a finger through the carved loops in the bed's footboard. "You're the one with the money."

"You know"—Luca pushed himself forward with his hands, putting his face inches from the immortal's—"before you came in, I was hoping an anvil would fall from the sky and put me out of my misery, and now you want me to *think*?"

"Actually, I was trying to make you laugh."

"Pfft." But Luca's face cracked into a smile despite himself as he sank back into his pillows.

It took some more debating about amount and explaining the exact location, but after half an hour, the servant who'd answered the bell call was off down into the city with its traffic, canals, and obsession with red. Kennet felt a rush of breath expand his lungs as his muscles started unclenching. *Step two accomplished.* Tea, he needed tea.

As if reading his thoughts, Luca jerked his head to a tray hunkered on a small table in the shadows by the wall. "Help yourself. You've been doing enough talking to dry out a swamp."

Well, maybe not so much talking as scheming. Kennet watched the prince as he started pouring tea from a slim, clear decanter. The glass was only lukewarm to the touch. But the scent wafting up to him was the distinct, sweet smell of a Camrai black. It didn't need to be hot to be savored. "Does Your Highness want any?"

Luca gave a sharp shake of his head. Whatever distraction Kennet had given the prince seemed to have evaporated far too quickly.

"Do you need your physician?"

Luca didn't answer, not with words, but the withering look that passed over his thin face was reply enough. He shifted and pulled himself deeper into his pillows. "I haven't slept all night," he said, his voice muffled by silk and down. "So, as punishment for waking me just as I finally dozed off, tell me something. Tell me about this flames-blasted book of lady's things I just spent a knight's ransom on. What's the story?"

Easing himself back into the seat by the bed, Kennet swirled the tea in his hand. Even the cup was in the Camrai style, a short glass fluted into the shape of a lazy hourglass. He took a long sip.

"Hmm, don't you know that story?"

There was no answer from the bed. The only sound was Luca's breathing. A labored but level thing, the sound of someone overwhelmed but not yet overrun.

"Well..." Kennet's eyes fell to the shadows that played in the dim light flickering across the headboard. They danced like bygone days. Real but fragile.

"The *story* goes that after centuries of division and conquest, the Albidoni finally united under two heroes, one from Varr and the other from the south in Iarla. Two lovers, it's said. Adile and Gillan were their names.

"They fought for years against the Swans of the Isles and the dragon riders of Atherland until one day the final battle came.

"Swan invaders had been sweeping through Varr, pushing westward until they were all the way to the River Lyr right at the border with Iarla.

"Both Adile and Gillan were on the field that day. Gillan on the Varr side of the river and his sweetheart with her forces on the other. She was supposed to join him, bringing her army over under cover of darkness. But before they could cross, Swan men destroyed the bridge, cutting Iarla off from Varr, dividing Albidon once again.

"As the battle began the next morning, Adile could do nothing but watch across the swollen, raging waters as her beloved and his men were cut down.

"But then—" Kennet paused, glancing up to the ceiling as if trying to push away memory of the facts and only tell the fiction, the *story*.

"As she watched," he finally went on, "she started to sing. One by one, the others by her side joined her, until every man and woman there east of the river was singing. Their voices rising up, clashing against the shouts and screams on the other side.

"What happened next, so the story goes, says that their song became so strong, filled with such power, that even the crystals growing in the caves far under their feet shattered at the force of the song, shooting up through the ground and into the air, piercing the enemy like a hail of arrows.

"Albidon won her freedom that day and crowned Adile and Gillan as their first king and queen. On the spot the battle was fought, the two built their capital, Odetown, forever uniting a divided land. The symbol the new king chose for his house was that of a lion in honor of his wife's mighty voice."

With that, Kennet fell silent. Even though his breathing insinuated he was still awake, Luca mercifully made no comment on the very un-united current state of Albidon.

Quietly, Kennet traced a finger along the rim of his tea glass. Truth, a bit of lie, a twist or two of fantasy, that's how history was remembered. Even he, in some ways, had forgotten how the real tale of Albidon's first king and queen had gone. He had been there, after all. So many centuries ago. But the diary last night had been a reminder of the true tale.

Seeing it had reminded him of something else, as well. Slowly his finger began to trace something new. Something with wings, something flying free, always free.

Though House de Glas may have chosen a lion, Adile's symbol—

That had been a nightingale.

THREE

DESMOND

Masque, Vawdawr Region
The same day

They say if you think sunny thoughts on a rainy day, there will always be a warm light in your soul. *They* have never been to the Masque. At least, not in late spring.

Desmond had seen rain often enough in his twenty-seven years, but not rain like this. It fell from the grey sky in streams neither light nor heavy. It was more like the miserable drip of a leaky bucket that had been left on too narrow a ledge.

All of it was a good match for Desmond's mood. He'd docked in the imperial city eight days ago and was steadily starting to feel more made of mildew than flesh and bone. But today, the sun had returned. It was peeking between the clouds in darting fits. Bright light traded with shadows across the embassy's foyer walls as fast as cards in the hands of a dealer.

"You're too thin. Both of you."

Desmond stopped chewing and swallowed before he was ready.

"Excuse me?" His eyes left his plate and followed a straight line down to the end of the long table. The table, a giant, carved thing made of mahogany, was normally meant for council meetings and treaties. But today, it was meant for breakfast—and its length was still not long enough to separate the captain from his guest.

"I said"—the woman at the other end rose and started to pace, each step bringing her closer—"you and Artair, you both look like foot soldiers on rations. Didn't your country's revolution bring the boon of royals down to the nobles? Seems more like the nobles tumbled right down into commoner's squalor." She paused by his chair and gave him a hard look that could only be defined as *judgment.*

Desmond took a swallow of water, then drained every mint-spiced ounce of it. "Equality goes many ways," he finally said. There was no use in giving a real answer.

Desmond hadn't been alive when noble houses like the Seymeres and d'Argons had overthrown Albidon's king decades ago. But he knew Lord Sebastian d'Argon had gotten enough glory from the event to eventually land a rich Vawde wife, one who was now staring down her nose at her son's captain.

Artair's father had died before his son had been born and his widow had only stayed in her husband's homeland long enough to give birth, then she had left, never to return. But if Sebastian d'Argon hadn't explained Albidoni thought on equality and freedom to his wife in the brief few years they'd been wed, well, Desmond wasn't volunteering.

Lady Valentina had passed the table now, but Desmond could still feel her dark eyes boring through him like a termite. Artair tended to keep things like seas and other people between himself and his mother. Desmond was beginning to understand why.

"You need a wife, Edenry." The contessa's voice came from near the hearth now. Even in late spring, a small fire blazed inside it. Anything to keep away the damp of the canals.

Desmond picked up a roll, one without butter or jam. He didn't have time for those things. He stuffed it into his mouth. Better to look like he had no manners than to reply and remove all doubt. This time he savored the experience until he was ready for it to end. If people wanted him to add things like pounds to his body or a wife to a marriage license, he needed time.

His uncle certainly hadn't given him any. He'd always known his mother's brother was rich, but some other unfortunate would be the heir—he'd assumed. In the twelve days since getting that black-ribboned letter, nothing had yet soothed the upheaval in his mind over all the things shoving him further and further from any concept of the word *good*.

He wasn't in the Falcons by conscription. He could leave if he wanted to, but throughout this foreigner's war, he'd kept holding on to the hope that it would end and he could go back to the life he had been planning: the path of a soldier, noble and true.

But as more and more cities fell and innocents died, that dream was starting to meld into a nightmare, one that felt irredeemable. And this? He reached for another roll. Maybe the only way out was to sell the estates and wash his hands clean of at least the gold. The blood though, that would never—

A servant leaned into the doorway. "My lady, your gondola has arrived."

Desmond rose, flipping his napkin up onto the table. "Didn't you want to speak to Artair?" he said, turning to the contessa. But she brushed past him with a single wave of a jewel-spangled hand.

"No, I will come again. Good day, Edenry." Pausing, she cast him one final look. "But tell him, I will come. I want my grandson educated here and that daughter-in-law of mine is stonewalling me."

I wager the d'Argons thought you were a real treat as an in-law, too.

But visibly, Desmond merely spread his lips into what passed as a smile and dropped a bow. As soon as the embassy's great doors shut, he sank back into his chair and let out a sigh. The relief lasted less than half a heartbeat.

"I've been robbed! Robbed! Robbed!" The words echoed off the stone walls in cadence with the clattering sound of footsteps.

What in the— Desmond shoved away from the table, kicking the chair over in his haste. Artair had a booming voice loud enough to wake the dead. His men liked to joke that he should be quieter on the battlefield. But today, as Desmond rounded the corner that led to the main landing, the sound had a tone more like bells tolling in alarm.

Long-fingered hands grabbed him before he'd made it two steps more, Artair's forward momentum pulling him almost completely around before both men came to a stumbling halt.

"I've been robbed," the lordling managed to gasp out one more time.

"Of your sanity?" Desmond swatted the hands away. "I'd believe that."

Artair ignored him. "Is she gone?" He craned his head backwards, peering into the room Desmond had just left. Seeing no one, he snapped straight again, planting his nose mere inches from his captain's. His hair looked like it had been washed then dried with raking fingers for a towel. And everything else about his dress spoke of haste, mayhem, and a touch of colorblindness.

Desmond was used to it. "What in the name of sense, man?"

Artair shook out his cuffs and ran a soothing hand down the front of his breeches as if smoothing the rumpled fabric would settle whatever situation he was about to spit out.

"The diary. It's gone."

"You have a diary?" Desmond couldn't keep the incredulous teasing from his voice. "I thought you just said everything you were thinking."

"Not mine," Artair ground back. "The Queen Mother's. Seymere gave it to me before we left, like a good luck charm, you know. The point is, he didn't give it to de Glas—"

"Obviously," Desmond cut in.

"And now it's gone!" Artair flung out his hands.

Desmond crossed his arms against his chest. The move was somewhere between disinterest and self-defense against his friend's still-swinging appendages. Artair had all the organizational talent of a manic tornado. The book was somewhere. *Lost.* Not stolen. If Desmond were at the card table right now, he'd bet his entire newfound fortune on this fact. *Now, there's a thought—*

"I know exactly what's going through that brain of yours and I'm telling you—"

"Ari's right. Des is wrong. Oh, what a day!" A new voice with its sing-song alto tone came from above, directly above. Desmond looked up just in time to see a figure made of silk and feathers drape her arms over the balustrade. There was a half-smile on the woman's impish face, a signature smile that belonged to only one person.

"Rhym." The name hissed out from between Artair's clenched teeth in the half heartbeat it took him to shove past Desmond and start up the stairs. Desmond followed at a slower pace. If life were a book, he'd read this scene before...many times.

Once upon not long ago, there had been three children: two boys and a girl. Their feet had scored tracks through the Albidoni dirt as they played their games and had their fun. But then they'd grown up and life had pulled them onto its own paths.

One had taken his position as county lord and country hero; the other had taken up his sword. And the girl? She had thought she would go with the lord, but then he had chosen another to join him on his new path. So, she'd left. Stolen goods, snatched secrets, that was now the game of Isadore Rhym.

"How'd you get in?" Artair's tone was as stiff as a brick wall when Desmond finally caught up, stepping into the small bookshelf-riddled little room he remembered his friend falling asleep in last night.

"Same way I did about a dozen hours ago," Isadore answered. "Well." She traced a thoughtful hand over a trio of violet pleats that graced the side of her dress before settling herself in a swish of silk on the window's curved seat. "I had to wiggle a little more this time. But all the same." She threw her shoulders up in an elegant shrug.

"Why?" For a man who would probably still be talking when he was a corpse, Artair could sometimes be brutally blunt. That's how you knew the man was angry.

Isadore's face had the decency to turn solemn. Her hands slid up to brace themselves against both sides of the arch that framed the window. Desmond took a step closer. He'd known Isadore long enough to know the sudden change in her mood had nothing to do with Artair. There was something else. She glanced over her shoulder out the window.

"I've seen a dead man," she started, her naturally low voice dipping even lower, a whisper-tone as if what she was about to say she wanted no one to hear, no one including herself. But she kept speaking anyway. "We got a job from Ink and Quill. I didn't have a choice. Steal back the Queen Mother's diary, those were the instructions—"

"They could have just asked for it," Artair cut in. He wasn't whispering. In fact, his tone seemed raised so whoever had commissioned this madness might hear and be ashamed by just sensing the sharp bite of his frustration. Isadore shushed him with a snap of her fingers. She threw another glance over her shoulder.

Desmond sighed. If this scene was going to play out like all the others that had come before it, Artair and Isa were about to be quarreling like two tomcats, the actual origins of their tussle as lost and forgotten as a bald grandda's brush. Besides—

"What do you mean, 'a dead man'?" he asked, stepping forward, hand unconsciously wrapping around the falcon-headed hilt of his sword.

Isadore's eyes remained locked with Artair's. She loved fighting as much as he liked talking. Desmond slid his sword up in the scabbard a few inches then let it fall back. The sharp click as metal kissed metal finally rewarded him with Isa's full attention. He gave her an impatient-encouraging circular wave of his hand.

"My client met me as we'd agreed," she began. "I could tell by the way he was dressed that he was the guild's current lord. When I asked his name, he said 'Kennet Zur.'"

Artair snorted, but Desmond took a step closer. "The Immortal Chronicler?" he asked, his eyebrows flaring with sudden interest.

But Isa's gaze was on Artair. "Look, I know what you're thinking—"

"Kind of your job, isn't it?" Artair had rounded the desk and was easing his long frame into the overstuffed chair. His downcast eyes bored into the papers scattered before him as if willing the diary to just reappear.

"I thought the same thing. This is just someone lost in the aura of his job. Swept away with the history and pomp of claiming to be someone who died centuries ago. But he'd been stabbed. *Over the heart*." Isa punctuated her words by standing and folding her arms across her chest, one hand fisted against her left breast.

Artair's gaze flickered up to her. "So, you stole something entrusted to me by the Unmaker himself and gave it to a now-dead man? Have you done anything else stupid in the past week?"

"I think what Isa is trying to say—"

"What I'm *saying*"—Isadore cut into Desmond's words like a scalpel into bare flesh—"is what you're thinking. He left, he died. I had to get the book back before some outsider took it. But then one of my boys told me it'd been sold already.

"So, I went to the place. A little black market shoppe on the southend by the quay. They said what I was looking for was already gone. When I asked for the description of whoever had sold the book to them, it was the same as my client's. *Exactly* the same. The shoppe owner was old, probably close to a hundred and a half, and he said he'd been working with the man for as long as he could remember. He looked at me almost shocked that *I* was shocked. Like—"

"Like we don't believe our own stories." Desmond rounded on his heel, setting himself at an angle to face the room's two occupants.

"Don't encourage this one, Rhym," Artair sighed. "He believes in all the things. Even the bogeyman."

"Nightmares are real," Desmond replied, his voice void of anything but flat fact. It was one thing to be Albidoni and hear stories spun and told. It was quite another to actually believe them.

Desmond was a practical man. He owned precisely seven changes of clothing to match the seven days of the week, and he believed in exactly one dozen stories, no more, no less.

One of those stories was that of the Immortal Chronicler, the half-blooded Albidoni sent back by God from death centuries ago to live out the rest of history chronicling the world's greatest tales. It wasn't a role passed down from man to man. It was the reality of only one man. And he was *here*.

Desmond felt his mind let out a little squeak at the thought. He might not have been the boy wanting to tell stories, but boy, man, knight, heir...he still loved to hear them told. If he had the habit of making wishes, listening to the Chronicler tell his tales live in person, now that would be something worth casting a ha'penny into a fountain for.

Artair was not so easily swayed. "There are many men who look alike. Ink and Quill probably has some standards for their masters. Qualifications in looks and so on."

Isadore swatted the excuse away with a flip of her fingers. "There are very few men in this world who are nigh seven feet tall."

"Ha! See, you owe me something." Desmond's hands found his hips. "Pretty sure we had a bet about this at some point."

Artair's own hands landed on the desk's top with a smack, scattering letters into even more disarray. His angular face twisted into a grimace as if the taste of admittance was a complicated thing. "Fine, *fine*. But I'll have to borrow the money from you first."

"Oh, about that. Congratulations, Edenry." Isadore turned her signature smile Desmond's way. Unlike its usual mood, sincerity graced the expression this time.

But Desmond didn't return the favor. The mention of his unplanned misfortune brought him solidly back to earth, a wet, soggy one littered with gold coins. "Do you say that to all men at their funerals?" he muttered, eyes settling on a knothole in the floorboards.

"All right, let's suppose that some—" Artair waved a hand to measure an indeterminate number of years. "Some man's been wandering around for centuries writing down all the stories in our great, revered Library. Why have you rob me? Why not just ask? Unless—"

Artair stood far too quickly. Desmond's gaze was still lifting from the floor when the lordling started to pace, his words and eyes directed at Isadore. He huffed. "Do you suppose he wants the de Glas back in power?"

"Tell him to take it up with Parliament," Desmond interrupted. "Besides, what's a chronicler care about politics? The wilder the times, the better the tale." Suddenly, he felt very torn between defending one he felt was the world's best historian and one he knew to be the best of friends.

Isadore shrugged. "Oh, I don't know. If I was over a thousand, I might think it was my place to start meddling in everyone's business."

"What's your excuse now, then?"

"I heard that, d'Argon."

Desmond ignored them both. "There is a story, though," he started, his index finger flickering between waving at thin air and tapping against the tip of his chin. "The de Glas united Albidon and took the throne after the last Swan conquest, yeah?"

He didn't wait for affirmation. "It's said, the Immortal had traveled Albidon for twenty years before that, testing all the great families to find which one was worthy to rule the country.

He pitted them against each other with trials and games." Desmond wasn't sure who he was helping or defending by saying all this. "Supposedly, the de Glas most won his approval and that's how they became our royal family."

"So, you're saying," Isa said, "that he could be doing that again? Seeing if he thinks we need our kings or if we can truly let our choices and our heroes rule us? Take something important to our heritage. See which side goes for it first and hardest?"

Desmond just answered with a heave of his shoulders.

"So, we play his game. We get the diary back. How hard can that be?" Artair had circled around Isadore and taken her seat at the window. He sat it like a king on a throne. Except he wasn't one. He never would be. He was just the hero the Albidoni looked to today. They could find another tomorrow. That was their choice. A choice it seemed the eldest of their citizens was calling into question. *Chords, the* eldest.

"Hard in two ways. First, the one to purchase the Queen Mother's diary was the fourth prince imperial. It's in the palace."

Artair let out a whistle appropriate for the news. "Well." He ran a hand through his hair. "Might have to pull a few strings called 'Mother' if that's the case. But wait, doesn't this blow a hole in your grand theory?" He cast a look at both his captain and spymistress. "Why would the great"—he exaggerated the word—"Chronicler let his bait out of his sight?"

"It's not a hole, Ari. It's the proof," Isa replied. "The lord of Ink and Quill is currently employed by the imperial family, *specifically*, the fourth prince."

The room fell silent as each one became lost in an ocean of thought.

“Fine.” Artair finally stood, both levity and frustration draining from his face with each heartbeat. “There are no de Glas even in the city. I don’t see what kind of game this is going to be.” He shrugged. “But God made man free. Crowns put them in cages. We’ll remind our immortal friend of that. If we’re believing in bedtime tales in the daylight today, then it was always said the Chronicler was a man of the faith. He’ll see that God is on our side.”

“Pretty sure God is on his own side,” Desmond muttered under his breath, but even if he’d shouted, his words were lost in Isadore’s next statement.

“That’s the other problem.” Isa looked at both men in turn. “The de Glas, both of them, *are* in the city. As of last night, they’re here.”

FOUR

LAUDILAS

Laudilas de Glas, second commander of the Albidoni Third Light Infantry, loved geometry. More specifically, the study of the arching shadow a glass made against a wall as he drained it dry. It was only three hours past noon, but he was already surrounded by bottles. And he was on leave with orders straight from himself to empty them all.

Tonight was La Notte and every citizen in the Masque would be fueling their sin with liquid red. Laudilas was getting a head start. He was a prince, after all. "Royalty trumps the rabble," he muttered, tipping another swallow down his throat. He winced. He'd tasted better vinegar. But as long as it did its job. As long as it numbed out this foreign war and his brother's homeland ambitions, that was enough.

"Mother's mercy!" a voice called out from the street. A cart rattled by stacked high with red masks.

God was dead, at least that's what the Vawde believed. Nothing stood between man and the swinging scales of Death now. But Mother Death, she could be kind, they said. One night a year, a man's sins went unseen. Anything, everything was not counted against him.

Tonight was that night.

Laudilas, second son of an ousted royal family, didn't care. The Albidoni didn't follow the Mother. God was very much still alive. But they didn't care if you believed that or not. And for Laudilas, apathy was a religion itself. If God hadn't cared about enthroned kings, he definitely wasn't interested in disinherited princes. So, Laude was returning the favor. A blind eye for a blind eye.

Without looking away from the disappearing cart, he reached for another bottle. His fingers met a small glass instead. He didn't remember ordering whiskey. Still not looking, like a spontaneous gamble, he downed the little tumbler's contents.

Chords blast it all! A taste even more bitter than the wine but somehow heavier and thicker met his senses. The liquid was down his throat before his mind's screaming could stop it.

Coffee.

He whipped his head from the tavern's window. If flames could have jumped from his eyes, he would have lit his brother on fire.

Benerict had claimed the seat opposite his at the table and was looking at him. Just looking. Benerict was good at that. It was like he'd been born with the notion that if he stared long enough at a world that had rejected his family and taken their crown like candy from a naughty child, someone might just give it back.

It hadn't worked. All the eldest de Glas had gotten for his trouble was an army, one that gave him just enough glory to keep Albidon's royalist remnants happy. But everyone knew both Benerict and the men under him were pawns of the rebels who now controlled their country.

But then, four years ago, the Imperator had sent out the call to Albidon. His navy had protected their shores for two centuries. It was time for the Albidoni to return the favor. Send their men over the sea. Kill the Chanti.

Even the Golden Godsent had been forced to pack up his Falcon knights and answer the call. The image of Artair's face as the gilded fool had realized the world was filled with chess boards, and even he was just a piece in the game of greater men flickered through Laude's memory. His lips curled into a smirk despite himself.

Benerict took it as an invitation to stop staring and finally open his mouth.

"The embassy was robbed last night."

"What embassy and why do I care?" Laudilas swatted the glass holding the last swig of coffee. It tipped to its side, and he watched with grim fascination as a stream of brown splattered down onto his brother's silver-toned armor. *Chords, does the man even know clothing exists?*

"Ours, of course."

Right, like anything else exists in the world besides Albidon.

"So, have you chased down the miscreants?" Laude drew a hand across his mouth, dragging the coffee taste away from his lips. "Clamped them in irons; gotten a confession? Has anyone thanked you yet?" He ticked off the rest of the list with his fingers. But Benerict was staring again. That special stare he reserved only for his brother. Translated, it was always some form of, *I was born to be a king. Idiots stand in my way, and my family are the greatest dunces of all.*

Laudilas was not like Benerict. The only match between the two men was their mother's ice-blue eyes and their father's surname. Benerict was raven-headed while Laude had the moonsilver hair House de Glas had always been famous for. But that was the only thing royal about him.

Today, yesterday, and fates willing, forever, Laudilas de Glas had no interest in caring if his ancestors had worn crowns on their heads or chains on their wrists.

Professionally, before the war, he had been a stage actor, a good one if Prevecost broadsheets were to be believed. But he'd also been trained to fight. Benerict had never given him an option there. So, here he was now exercising the baser of his talents in the Imperator's stupid war.

No matter how hard he tried, he kept finding himself trapped by the wants of men with crowns wrapped around their heads or their hearts. *Crowns are a cage,* the Albidoni freedom fighters had always said. Laude was pretty sure he believed them.

"No." Benerict finally blinked, his voice slicing into Laude's thoughts with that tenor pitch of his that was so out of place with everything else about him. "It was Queen Adile's journal that was taken and now it's been sold on the black market. Prince Luca's in possession as of two hours ago."

Even with the coffee racing now through his blood, Laude was still neither fully drunk nor anywhere near actually sober. So, his mind sputtered not once but twice as it flipped through a mental image of everyone foreign and domestic currently in the Masque that might bear the title of prince.

He came up blank.

"Fourth prince imperial," Benerict supplied. He leaned forward, locking his scarred hands on the tabletop. Even though he was a full inch shorter than Laude, that pose and the look that came with it was always a gate, one the younger de Glas had never found a way to break through. Yet. "He's crippled. Not many people have ever seen him, but he's not a recluse. Get it back."

Those last three words did more than internal submersion in a barrel of coffee. "What? Me?"

"You want d'Argon to get it?"

The sudden shift from near numbness to alertness sent a tremor through Laude's hands. Reaching up, he tangled his fingers into his long hair and started twisting strands into a braid. "He lost it. That's got to count for some embarrassment. Who cares if he's the one to get it back?"

"Because, if we return it home, it will show we care about our people's treasures. Heart of my heart, that sort of thing." Benerict tapped his breastplate with a knuckled fist.

Laude's eyes followed his brother's hand. Inset throughout Benerict's pale armor were swirls of scarlet, the color of House de Glas.

Laudilas snitched a small silken cord from a wine bottle that stood tragically full and started to tie off the end of his braid. His eyes trailed up to meet his brother's. Kingdoms rose and fell and dynasties with them. This was the truth of history. But the chronicles only told who won and who lost. Parchment and ink didn't bleed, not like hearts. Books never told the story of how the defeated carried their pain.

It had been over four decades since the Albidoni had overthrown their royal family, betraying them into the hands of the Athlanders. Queen Rhysana had offered a ransom, but with their king now where they wanted him, the Albidoni had never given a ha'penny to get him back.

The youngest royal child had been allowed to keep his title of prince and remain in his homeland. But he had become the pawn of the noble houses now in control of the country, and his own sons had inherited nothing but legacy.

Neither Benerict nor Laude were stupid enough to believe that their grandfather hadn't deserved his fate. And their own father had been weak. But Benerict was different.

People loved Artair, the young golden hero who'd risen up over the past decade to lead Albidon, because he was good. Benerict...well, he was yet another thing Laude was not. He was good, too. And still most Albidoni didn't want him. The haunting of it drove the would-be-king. *Someday, it's going to drive him straight into the arms of darkness.*

"Why can't you go?" Laude's voice felt faint and far away even to his own ears. He wasn't supposed to care. He was supposed to pick up his bottles and march upstairs to his room. His trunk was heavy enough to bar his door. And yet, he was still sitting there... *Maybe that chords-blasted stare does work and I'm the fool who's going to hand over the candy crown.*

Benerict shook his head. "All company leaders have been summoned by the Imperator to the Turrim to discuss the siege at Voorst—"

"What? No fun tonight? Come on, it's La Notte!" Laude huffed. "So, that means Artair will be there, too, then?"

Benerict gave a single nod.

"So?" Laude mirrored his brother's solitary movement with a one-shouldered shrug. "Both of you race for it tomorrow. Wait, does he even know where it is or do we have that advantage at least?"

Who is this we?

"Rhym's told the count everything—"

"I'm up against *Isa*?" If the answer had been yes, anything even near the country of yes, Laude was going upstairs and stuffing himself into his trunk.

But Benerict shook his head. "She's leaving. Burns saw her looking for passage at the east dock awhile ago. She'll be gone by sunset."

Laudilas let himself breathe. If Isadore Rhym was the Godsent's lapdog, Peet Burns was Benerict's hound. The two could make information dance like lightning between Albidon's royalist and nationalist sides. Both terrified Laude.

"Burns said the Falcon's captain is going. Lucky for you, that man has all the personality of warts. All you have to do is speak to the prince as one royal to another. His Highness will understand that language. Edenry doesn't have that advantage. However—"

"Desmond Edenry? He made captain?" Genuine surprise crossed Laude's face. He had seen the man just a few weeks prior. There had been no extra embellishment on that black and gilded armor to state his rise in rank. *That's Edenry for you.*

The knight Laudilas remembered was known throughout the teahouses of Albidon as having a mouth short on words, but a mind full of stiff-headed opinions. Anti-monarchist sentiment ran strong with that one.

Still, Laude had always liked him. Something about his raw-boned honesty was like a refreshing breeze—even if that breeze would happily have knocked both Laude and his brother into the sea.

"Yes." Benerict's face flattened deeper into a frown. "Unfortunately, he's just inherited the Thorne wealth. *All* of it."

"What's wrong with that? It's not like he's going to dump his own inheritance into paying off a political problem."

"It's Artair's political problem and Edenry only understands one emotion—loyalty. So, you have the edge of your rank. Edenry has his gold."

It took a moment, a dozen heartbeats, maybe two; even the bracketed hourglass dangling by a single brass chain from the ceiling seemed to mute the sound of its flow. Then Laudilas pushed away from the table. Even towering now over his brother, he still felt like he was kicking against a double-locked gate. But at least he could afford himself one consolation prize.

"If I do this," he said, hands splayed on the tabletop, "I do it my way."

The muggy sunlight that streamed in dusty trails across the tavern floor started to dim. In its place, shadows leapt from corners and started to tangle with the light. They licked up the walls, peaking in a phantom crown over Benerict's head. The few patrons at the other tables gasped and one bolted for the door.

Laudilas smiled. The Albidoni may have denied him his birthright, but they could not deny him everything. Albidon was the land of the loreborn, a people devoted to stories, to wishes, to illusion. Not every Albidoni was an illusionist, but those who were chose their affinity.

For Laude, it had been the easiest of choices. Shadows, phantoms, the echoes of nothing for a nothing prince.

He smiled again, this time at his brother. "I'll tell him a story—" He paused, another passing cart catching his eye. This one was like the first, piled high with red masks and streamers, one of which was unspooling from its hook and trailing down onto the cobbles like a trickling rivulet of blood.

Laude's lips twisted up even higher. "The one about the Sisters Six."

INTERUDE

WATER

Secrets. They were what was wrong with the world. The canal waters had been sure of this for centuries beyond recount. Still, they drank down man's hidden things like a greedy drunkard would his wine.

The Immortal. The Knight. The Brother.

As each one's heartbeat drew him closer to nightfall, the waters had been watching, hungry to know it all.

The Immortal had a plan. The waters could smell it in the determined way his footsteps had struck the puddle-pocked flagstones of the high street as he left the palace just as the mid-morning hour had rung out throughout the city.

He was being followed.

It had started with the spymistress. *Isadore?* The name sounded right as the waters rolled it between them in small splashes. Since the woman hadn't found the dead body she'd seemed so sure was slumped out there somewhere, her lackeys had been out searching for the diary before dawn.

Perish forbid something be twice-stolen in less than a day, wave whispered to wave.

It hadn't taken Isadore long to find the clues Kennet had taken little care to cover up.

Kennet Zur wasn't one of those immortals people liked to invent for fanciful tales. He didn't have a network of spies and servants who kept their roles generation after generation. He managed with what he could find in the moment.

It usually worked. When someone taller than most rooms in the slums came by offering both money and instructions, people typically didn't waste time asking, *says who?*

So, it had been easy enough to find willing mouths to let slip all the little details as the diary had changed hands from the Immortal, to the Givannos, and finally to the fourth prince.

The fact that Kennet hadn't even glanced behind him as he'd left the palace told the waters that the crippled prince would probably never get to see the book. Maybe Kennet cared a little, but not hardly enough to alter his course now. The plan was flowing like a gondola cradled in the hands of a willing current.

If things continued on this way, the ancient queen's ink-splotched diary would be back in Albidoni hands by midnight.

The only question that remained was just exactly which ones.

The waters of the Masque tasted everything they took. The scraps of broken treaties, the tarnish of stolen treasure, and every willing or unwilling body that came to them. Some things the waters hoarded forever, their mysteries slowly peeled away and then abandoned over time. But others the waters spat back. Some things, even drowned or dead, spelled trouble for those still above the surface.

Along some stradas, the canal water was brown, filled with churned mud. On others, the color was the darkest green. But no matter what substances threaded through their waves, all the canals of the Masque loved one thing most of all—trouble.

And the kingdom of Albidon had always been the most delicious kind of trouble.

Divided into regions and small city-states for most of its existence, it hadn't been until the rise of House de Glas that the loreborn had finally united as one. But like the members of a choir who can't agree on even the time of day, the national harmony hadn't lasted long.

But the waters had known better than to expect it to.

All nations had been gifted at the Dawn in their own unique ways. The Immortal's father's people had been the Veil, blessed with great wisdom. To the Vawde, who made up most of the current citizenry of the Masque, had come the power of governance and order. And across the seas: east, south, and west were other kingdoms, each with their own singular gifts.

But in Albidon, that crooked little peninsular land just to the north of the Satin Sea, to them the Almighty had given stories. All that man was in the beat of his heart, the thoughts of his mind, all the way down into the wishes hidden deep within his soul.

Most other nations saw the gift as frivolous: the Albidoni were just a kingdom of minstrels and playwrights, producers of mankind's leisure at best and waste of time at worst. But some over the centuries had come to realize the terrifying truth of the people they called the loreborn.

To create, man must be like water. In some measure, large or small—he must be free.

So, the loreborn were singers, dancers, artists. Rebels.

A small wave caught a piece of round silver as it tumbled from the Immortal's pocket down into the canal with a plink. It was a new one. The wave could tell as its tongue met the phantom space where a crown had once been part of the coin's design. *God made man free.* The ancient Albidoni mantra was now etched in the crown's place.

But before the wave could explore its new threat further, a hand struck through its crest, snatching the coin away and scattering the wave from one into three.

"Thief." Kennet snorted, cupping his coin as his tall frame cast the water into shadow. The three waves shook their heads, jetting away from him, reaching for the sunlight beyond. But just ahead, spanning the Grande Via, was a bridge, its stone and steel weight belting the sun-cloaked water in darkness.

The time. Somehow the water had lost track of the Immortal. And how he was here, and the sun was fading westward fast.

As if in spite, a spray of water dropped down from the bridge, splashing Kennet on the cheek. The Immortal pulled his hand away from the coin and caught the next drops before they could land. The water that pooled in his palm was the rusted color of old blood.

Really, it was just runoff from last night's rain mixed with decay from the bridge's metal underpinnings. The canal knew this. But, here in this city, it might as well have been someone's river of life.

The Vawde were not like the loreborn. They valued order. But ever since Darkness had come and the world had fallen into him so many millennia ago, that love of order had warped and twisted itself into dominance and a hunger for power, a hunger that could not be sated.

This new millennium, not even two decades old, had brought what House Drake was calling the *Seconda Gloria*. Glory, triumph, and empire reborn.

Kennet watched as the water drained into his skin, leaving a dirty ring in the center of his hand. A ring like the link in a chain.

A man can be both master and slave. People didn't tend to believe this, but the waters knew it was true. They had tasted it again and again.

It was hard to say exactly how it had begun. In whispers most likely. But one thousand years ago, as the remnants of this city had grieved for their dead, a religion had been born.

Maybe it was peace the Vawde had wanted, certainty in the midst of ruin. Whatever they'd been looking for, they'd found it in the hands of Death—or so the tossed, old scrolls had claimed as their ink had melded with the water. The Dark Sister's heart bled for the fallen and so she became a mother to the living. If they served her well, she would remember their deeds and when their time came, she would be their advocate before the Darkness.

God is dead. Darkness reigns. May the Mother have mercy.

It sounded lovely. Lies were always sweetest in the first bite. And so, link by link, soul by soul, year by year, the religion had grown.

But as it grew, one thing had become clear—there was no mercy, not for those who didn't follow. At first, it was just small things like a scornful look between two former friends, a missed business opportunity. But then the blood began to flow. The people of this city were creating canals of their own, ones running red.

It was Kennet who had bled first.

PhantomRin.

FIVE

KENNET

Sickle and scythe. Truth and lies. Mother mine, red as wine. Will you save me now?

Kennet listened to the child's song fade as the little one's figure disappeared down the canal. He was standing at the base of a bridge where three of the Masque's main waterways converged into the Grande Via.

Despite his looming presence, people didn't seem to notice him as they walked or rowed past. Humans were good at that, he'd observed over the years. Most could hope to live a century and a half if they were lucky, and all that time, they'd be looking in corners for dusty whispers and nonsense while the flat truth stared them in the face, hounding their steps, too often ignored to the last breath.

But at least there was some action today. Half a dozen of his countrymen had pulled their heads out of whatever dark places they normally kept them and had been making tracks across the city since early morning.

Kennet sighed as he settled his shoulders more deeply against the stone molding of the bridge wall. From this vantage, he could see straight into the Rex and Rod across the narrowest channel in the waterway.

Both de Glas brothers sat at a table by the tavern's wide window, deep in conversation. If Kennet were a comic artist for the broadsheets, he knew exactly how he'd depict these two. One didn't know where he ended and the glass crown began, and the other had a similar issue with wine bottles.

The moonsilver-haired princeling reminded the immortal a little of his younger self. The thought wasn't a compliment to either of them.

He scrubbed his palm against the leather of his breeches, rubbing away the rusty mark that ringed in the center of hand. But nothing could erase the memories rising up in his mind.

It had all started here. He'd been born in this city, born a bastard, growing up wild and free. But it had all ended here as well. Ended with a mistake. He'd only been sixty-eight, just barely past the halfway mark of life. He wasn't even a Vawde citizen by that point, but still, one night, guards dressed in red uniforms that looked like they'd been taken from a tailor's mold before being truly finished had broken into his rented flat and dragged him away.

Less than twenty-four hours later, he was dead.

"Rude, rude, rude," Kennet muttered. The images, the pain, phantom now but real once, sent energy shooting down into his legs. With a grunt, he gave the wall a side kick. Then, sliding up his hood, he stepped out from the shadow of the bridge.

The afternoon breeze was fitful, but as he cleared the last step that led up from the waterway to the high street above, a gust blew the hood back, slamming it firmly onto his shoulders.

He left it.

Usually, he found humor in the twisted reality that he didn't actually have to hide in this city. The matriarchs who ruled as the Mother's voice and hands were so set on believing God was dead that they couldn't fathom a deceased deity bringing anyone else back from under the sod.

Another thing no longer on their list of probabilities was the execution of other kingdoms' visiting citizens. Kennet may have been the first to die in this city for believing what he wanted and not what he'd been told. But he had been the last foreigner.

It was a good thing.

It was a problem.

People didn't tend to notice blades unless they were biting into their own necks.

Kennet didn't doubt that more than one Albidoni had noticed over the years that the Masque liked its executions about as much as other governments liked taxes. But they were busy, busy like bakers testing a recipe, trying to find just exactly what circumstances would make them the most comfortable, the freest.

Somehow over the years, though, their experiments had risen like an over-yeasted loaf, blinding them to everything but themselves.

Even with the Rex and Rod behind him now, Kennet could still feel the tension of the eldest de Glas, his obsession with the crown.

And the other players in this game weren't much better. Kennet had checked in on them earlier.

He could sense that Isadore had finally caught up with him as he'd left the palace. But with legs as long as his and years of experience in the city that stretched out even longer, he'd managed to outpace her, circling around until he'd become the hunter instead of the prey.

She had led him to the Albidoni embassy, just like he'd expected. Maybe the conversation that ensued inside was supposed to be quiet, but watching from the balcony of the building's abandoned neighbor, Kennet had gotten the gist of most of it.

Freedom! No kings. We make the rules. Oh, chords, there might just be *an Immortal after all.*

Something like that.

If he were to portray Isadore's two companions in caricature, it might go along the lines of a lordling cupping a glass filled with pure sunshine in one hand while the other held a double-edged sword ready to impale anyone who tried to take it away.

The other was a solemn but more interesting man, a captain with a full cup too. The color inside his cup was indeterminate, but it didn't matter. The captain was certain the contents were a potent hemlock, out to poison everyone. The fervor of trying to keep one single drop from touching anything, anyone that was innocent and right had burned him down like a candle left to blaze too long.

Kennet pitied the man. Someone like him might once have been the answer to Kennet's plan, the piece that fit in the puzzle so well, it would make his eyes bulge.

But not now. As the trio's conversation had taken a downspin into who was going after the book, when they were going, and the occasional repeat of *why* they were going, it became clear—the captain wasn't interested.

Kennet couldn't catch his exact arguments. There had been some shouting, some door slamming, then Isadore had left and both men had quickly followed. Where they were going didn't matter to Kennet now.

Just before the conversation had gone from neat yolks to scrambled, he'd caught the announcement he had been waiting for—

"The de Glas, both of them, are in the city."

That bit of news had led him to the bridge and the Rex and Rod. And now here he was walking without purpose or aim down the length of the high street. When it ended, he kept on, his feet turning onto a narrow, dipping footpath that edged out along a side-canal pocked with lily pads.

The sun above was fading towards sunset. Its golden rays skimmed over the westernmost towers and spires of the city, casting the east into shadow. Tonight was coming.

Nothing would happen. The point of this game wasn't to manically wave centuries of injustice in the face of a few handpicked loreborn and hope they would suddenly spring to life and slay the metaphorical beast, bringing hope and freedom for all with the dawn.

This wasn't surgery, this wasn't the cure. Not yet. Kennet had been gone a long time. Far away. In that century, a generation had risen and faded into old age. He needed to test the pulse of his mother's people anew.

Freedom had always been what drove them. But now, it seemed that they were obsessed with which side treasured and promoted the ideal best. To some, like the count and his captain, kings were the killers of free spirits and, by default, stories. But to others in Albidon, a royal family was the greatest story of all, the stuff legends were made from. How could they be true to themselves if they were not faithful in every part?

Seeing which of them might come for a treasure that had belonged to the mother of their nation would tell Kennet something. He would study why they came and how. He would watch them over the next half a dozen hours like a teacher looking over his pupils to see which were ready for the next task.

Tonight was for him.

Heaving a sigh that matched the rhythmic croak of a frog staring at him from the nearest lily pad, Kennet dropped onto a small stone bench.

Someday, maybe, at least one loreborn would see with clear eyes the tyranny in this city. Only freedom had power over slavery's chains. The people of stories could bring that. *Could* being the operative word.

Would being the terminal question...

He kicked at a small stone. The light here was dim, blocked by high palazzo walls on all sides, but as the stone skipped towards the water's edge, it glinted. Not a stone then. A coin.

Kennet's head spun around, his shoulders brushing against something hard and cold behind him as he did.

The unmoving, carved face of a statue met his eyes. A statue of the Mother.

Unlike the high spired sancts of Albidon and the Veil, or even the looming temples of the Camrai gods, the little statued alcoves of the Mother snuck up on a person like a viper in tall grass.

"Fall and ruin," he breathed. Another sigh, this one shaky, slipped from his lips then was cut off as his throat clenched into something between a laugh and a hard swallow.

The frog on the lily pad was staring harder now, its bulging eyes taking in both Kennet and the statue behind him that his tall frame all but dwarfed...and yet somehow didn't at all.

But then its eyes bulged larger. Its mouth opened to croak, but no sound came out. With a leaden *thunk*, the creature vanished under the water, lily pads scattering as it fell.

In that instant, Kennet felt the coolness of the marble behind him turn colder. Not the sort of chill that went to the bone, but one that could stop a heart, freeze a breath, end a life.

"Annoying creature." The voice behind Kennet cracked through the air like a scourge then slowly bled towards his left ear as it went on. "Its time should have been up days ago. Hello, Immortal."

Kennet's legs shoved him to his feet and his neck turned to face the voice now directly beside him. But he was numb. The cold leached into his bones, his mind, his veins, reaching scraping fingers for his beating heart. Then it stopped.

The voice snorted. "Bah, you're no fun."

What had been a pale and slender statue robed in vibrant red mere seconds before was now a raven-haired warrior clad in shadows thick as scales. She moved to stand before him. Her, the Dark Sister, the Grey Hand, the Pale Mercy, the Red Lady. So many names, so many colors for one final, terrible thing—

Death.

"Come to celebrate my holiday, hmm? I'm flattered." She gave him a wicked wink, hoarfrost-tipped lashes scraping against her pallid skin.

Kennet's hand gripped at his heart. Even as the cold and numbness retreated, even though he knew he couldn't die—not again—still, the power of the figure before him was overwhelming. No man could stand against Death, not forever. All men came to her in the end.

And yet— And yet that was the thing, wasn't it?

"What do you want?" he finally asked, pulling himself straight and giving his cloak a shake as if to brush off every inch that had touched the statue and the bench.

The Dark Sister threw up her shoulders in a shrug and jabbed a long finger his way. "You're the one sitting here in my alcove not even bothering to give me a ha'penny." She sniffed. "What was the word you used earlier? 'Rude.' Yes. That's what you are."

Kennet let his cloak hem drop. The sky overhead had darkened but this time it was thickening clouds that blocked the sunlight. A drop of rain splattered down onto the dirt path between them. A buzz of lightning crackled through the air, but it was Kennet's gaze that held the thunder.

He took a step forward. His hand flashed out. His fingers seized Death by the collar. With one spinning motion, he hauled her up and around, pinning her figure hard against the alcove's narrow side wall. The shadows of her armor licked through his skin and the icy barbs that ridged the scales every few inches cut him deep, but he didn't let go.

Her breath puffed in the air the color of sooty smoke. "No reason to get angry," she grunted, straining against the strength of his grip. "I'm just doing my job. Just like you do yours." She planted both of her hands over his, her fingers chilling until they looked more like ice shards than flesh.

"Ah, but that's the thing, isn't it?" Kennet ignored the cold seeping into his hands. "You didn't do your job. Once. You couldn't." His lips twitched. "There is no dead Almighty, is there? Death can't keep what has never known sin. You failed; you had to let him go. The One Below wasn't very happy, was he? His grand plan all gone to hellfire." Kennet's brows flared in a questioning arch. But they both knew the answer.

"You see," Kennet went on. "I'm old enough to remember. When I was young, we called Darkness the One of Many Faces. But not here, here he was just himself, all that was not Light, all that was not God. Barefaced, plain darkness, no veil, no pretense. This city worshiped that. But now?" He spun the question in a circle with his free hand before pulling away. His feet paced backwards towards the canal.

"He's not afraid." Death was inches from Kennet's face in less than a heartbeat, her words coming out in a rasping rush. Her soulless eyes were black, the shadows of her garments wild and writhing around her. "He's not afraid," she repeated.

"If Darkness is so unafraid..." Kennet closed the distance between them. Around him, his cloak snapped in high-pitched twangs driven by the stormy breeze, but his voice had dipped low, the maelstrom of his feelings weighing it down. He shook a fist at the alcove, to the offerings scattered around the foot of the dais where the statue of the Mother had been. "Tell me," he hissed. "Why then is he wearing your face?"

The question hung between them, tipping back and forth in the wind like a sickle uncertain which direction to pierce.

"This isn't you." Kennet finally broke the silence. "You're right, you've got a job: passing man on to whatever eternity he's chosen for himself. But this? *This* is him. Another face. Another lie. Another trick. Few men are mad enough to fall at the feet of hell itself. But if that hell looks like heaven? Enough honey can make even vinegar sweet.

"And he's using you. It's man's choice where he goes, what he puts faith in. You've got nothing to do with it. There's no mediating mother standing between man and Darkness at the end. The only reason he likes that image is it puts him on the throne he's always wanted, the one he can never—"

"You act like I don't know this." Death cut into Kennet's speech with a stamp of her foot. Maybe on someone else the move would have looked childish, but as the ground shook beneath his feet, rattling his bones and sending ripples out into the canal water, Kennet found any other words frozen to his tongue.

She went on. "I was born the day man sinned, and I was put into the Dance with the others. Six sisters we are. But I'm not like Time or Wisdom; man does not love me or cherish me. But here?" Her colorless lips slid into a smile, the falling rain trickling down her face like a testament to every tear she'd ever made man shed. "Maybe I like it. But"—she flashed up a hand—"as you said, I have a job. I do not help *him*, and I will not help you. What is it, though?" Her hand suddenly fell to settle on Kennet's chest. But there was no chill in her touch this time, no grasping reach for his beating heart. Silently, she seemed to listen. "What is it you want, Immortal?" The gaze that met his was raw with curiosity.

What do I want? Wasn't it obvious? Freedom. Justice. A breaking of chains. But the question latched deeper. Kennet shook his head, water from his dark hair spraying in his face. There was nothing else. No other purpose...

But somewhere inside of him, something buried deep—ignored but not denied—whispered up in answer. *I'm here.* Its voice was quiet, subdued, but *hungry*. Kennet's shoulders suddenly slumped against the downbeat of the rain.

Death went on, her voice both questioning and knowing all at once. "Why are you here, playing this game with men—" She sniffed at the air. "Some of them, yes, I can feel it, some I will visit very soon. Maybe I won't take them then. But they are mortal. Maybe they will try at your mission; maybe they might fail. Even if you end this, there will only be another."

Her hand balled into a fist against his heart. "Many Faces, many faiths. Over and over again, until we have all danced the last measure there will be. So, what do you want? Do you care about people? Or do you want—"

A peal of thunder rolled overhead.

"Revenge?" The word slipped from the Dark Sister's lips just as her eyes cut away from Kennet's to the canal behind them.

"Listen, Immortal." Her eyes were back at his again, urgency this time flickering within their shadowy depths. Her voice had sunk from a rasp down into a whisper. "Whatever it is you want, whatever you plan to do—" She was fading, both in voice and body. But like an echo, Kennet caught her last words and her second glance at something behind him. "I'm not"—the words trickled into his ear—"I'm not the one standing in your way."

And then she was gone. Silent and red robed, a statue once more. Kennet slumped down onto his knees. Unlike her touch, which always faded with time, her words twisted through him still.

Why? Why?

"You. Chronicler!" The voice came from behind him. Loud, demanding, its accent indiscernible. Still disoriented, Kennet tried to stand but stumbled. Footsteps pounded behind him. Before he could try again, hands were grabbing him, pinning his arms in a grip tight as shackles.

"Unhand me!" Kennet jerked his body hard to the right, trying to yank away or catch a glimpse of his attacker. But the turn of his head only brought him in full sight of the canal. A lone gondola, its curtains mostly drawn, idled mere yards away from the alcove. Its approach must have been what had sent Death back so quickly into her marbled repose.

"Let me go," Kennet repeated, lunging forward and twisting his head around again. This time he managed a brief sight of his assailant. The man was like him, mountainous. But where Kennet might have been compared to a tall, singular peak, the span of this man's shoulders could have made up an entire range of impassable summits. His face was masked and his clothes so nondescript as to be a definition all on their own.

I'm not the one standing in your way.

Someone knew. Someone was here to stop him. Kennet turned to face the gondola again. But as he did so, a sack started falling over his eyes. He drew in a breath and started to toss his head like a stallion bucking off a rider. But the breath was a mistake. The sweet, toxic scent of bilberri swept through his nose, down his throat and up into his mind. The drug's power was like a dam, diverting thought, then cutting it off again and again, until all was still and silent.

As the darkness descended in a rush of night sweeping away both thought and vision, he caught just one glimpse of a single figure barely visible but still recognizable inside the shadows of the gondola's heavy curtains.

Him?

Shock surged through Kennet's ancient bones. Something he had not felt for a very long time. But before he could think a heartbeat further, the feeling collided with Death's still lingering question, and that answer...that feeling. That voice.

Why?

Over and over the words hammered and tumbled through his mind as his hands fell away from the vice grip that had held them and smacked against the ground. But just as unconsciousness took him, another word, something he'd seen just before his sight had been blocked, rose in one mighty swell before being cut off—

And then it was gone.

Phantom Rin.

SIX

DESMOND

"Are you mad! Or just trying out for the part?" Desmond was looking at Artair with all the consternation of a five-year-old who's just been told this year's Coming cake will feature squash.

"Just do this for me, will you?" Artair groaned, hands buried deep in his golden hair. He was slumped on the bottom stair in the foyer of the Masque residence of the late Gilbert Thorne. Now, the palazzo with its pale marble façade was Desmond's along with its problems—and the one Artair had been trying to stuff into his hands for the past hour.

With a weary heave of breath, Desmond sank down on the step beside his friend and leaned against the balustrade. It coiled down the two-story tall staircase like a sea serpent ending in a carved face that turned outwards as if ready to devour any who entered the front doors.

"Ari." Desmond's tone came out like another sigh or maybe just a continuation of the one before. "On my soul, I swear, I'd down a vial of alamander if it would help. But this?" His shoulders shuddered against a particularly sharp flare in the stair monster's neck.

Artair flickered a glance at him. Men swore by many things. To some the oath was serious. To others, vowing to the extreme was only a fanciful, dramatic gesture. But no one joked about alamander. Taken from al'am eels, it was the most agonizing poison known to man. It was used to kill, slowly, horribly. Victims weren't meant to survive and those few who did were driven insane by the torment.

Even as the words left his tongue, Desmond considered calling them back. He had felt for so long that he'd been set on a path that veined through the very hand of Death herself. Life had faded like the echo of a dream that may have never even been true.

But still, there was death...and there was death. A ghastly, terrible, poisoned death. But. His head twitched in an unconscious shake. No, he meant it.

Desmond didn't believe in kings. And he didn't put faith in heroes either. Not even Artair. Men were just men. But he did believe in brotherhood, loyalty, the promise of one to another to be a sword, a shield, whatever the other needed. Just not—

A fist pounded on the front door.

"You're supposed to answer that." Artair's dry tone was all but drowned out by the sound of flesh and bone hitting wood.

Desmond threw him an eye roll as another knock came, this one more insistent than the first.

Artair shrugged. "Your house, your door."

"Edenry," a voice came from outside. "I know you're in there."

Isadore. Leave it to the Lady of Black and White to climb through windows but bother to knock on doors.

"So," she began as Desmond finished spinning the lock loose and started tugging open one of the great carved doors. He held it wide enough to let in a slice of light, but not enough to give entrance to an entire woman.

Isadore took a step forward on the stoop. This close, Desmond had no choice but to take in a full inhale of her perfume. In the quantity it was being worn, it was more weapon than fragrance. Choking, he stumbled back, pulling the door further open. Exactly as she'd wanted.

"So," she repeated. "Have you decided?" Her smile was bright, but like her scent, there was too much of it. Tension lined her brow and twisted the upturned corners of her crooked lips.

"This one won't go and I can't. Meeting with the Imperator tonight," Artair said from where he still sat on the bottom step. He gave a general wave in Desmond's direction then stuffed his hands back into his curly hair.

"Why and why?" Isadore directed the trio of words at both of them before honing her gaze onto Desmond. "Scared, Edenry?"

Desmond slammed the door back shut with a side kick of his right foot and let out a snort that would have made any bull proud. "No." He took two steps towards Artair and met Isa's hard look with one of his own, his right eyebrow shooting up into an arch.

"I'm not scared. When you cut a man, his titles don't suddenly form an armor to protect him. All men bleed the same. I'm just no good at this sort of thing." He threw up his hands. "I'm not a speaker. I'm not charming and eloquent and—"

"You're doing plenty of talking right now," Isa cut him off. "Besides, money, Desmond, that's what you have to talk for you. Money. Chords knows you don't seem to want it. Luca Drake may be an imperial prince but titles don't mint coins for their bearers. Especially for a cripple. De Glas only has legacy. You know, 'my grandfather once bedded your great-aunt,' that sort of thing. And sentiment doesn't line pockets."

Desmond folded his arms so tightly against his chest, there was an audible squeak of leather against leather. "Which de Glas is going? You said more than one was in the city."

"Laudilas, the younger one. True, he's a charmer. He knows how to put on a show, but again"—she patted the pouch ribboned at her side—"talent doesn't jingle. Besides, I may have let it slip that you were the one going. Burns has been sniffing my heels all day and I wanted him to have something to go back and bay to his master about. So, go to save your pride if nothing else. But for heaven's sake, find something else to wear."

Isa's eyes traveled from Desmond's boots, past his black leather breeches, and over the long vest of matching leather, settling on his pale blue shirt. Prenz Leathers people called them, the off-battlefield uniform of the Falcon knights. "If you show up in that, it's going to send a wrong message."

"Pretty sure if he shows up *out* of it, it's really going to send the wrong message," Artair cracked.

Isadore rolled her eyes with enough force to flip the moon. "What do you know about clothes, d'Argon?"

Artair flashed a wide smile. "I wear them."

"Pfft."

Desmond scrubbed a hand over his face. The cry of souls and the scent of blood lingered as his fingers swept from cheek to jaw. Was that all his hand was destined for? To wield the whims of others as a weapon, first in steel and now in gold?

He squeezed his eyes shut. *For Artair. This is for Artair. He'd do the same for you. Granted, it'd go down with more dramatics and probably seven mistakes plus one more for good measure. But he'd do it and he'd win.*

The door shook on its hinges with the force of another knock. Desmond's eyes flew open. "Chords," he and Isa muttered in unison.

"You're supposed to get that," Artair said from where he still sat on the step.

"Yeah? Look what happened last time you said that and I opened the door." Desmond waved in Isa's general direction.

Isa acknowledged this by sweeping her skirts into a stage curtsy. "Blessings, yes."

Desmond had considered marrying Isadore once. He'd also once considered growing a mustache. Both ideas had ended up in a hole never to be resurrected.

He opened the door with a yank this time. Most of his uncle's servants had vanished for the day without a *please and may I*. Something about a holiday they were so in disbelief that their new master had never heard of, they'd thought he was joking. But even if one was returning, servants used the back door. This was the front. And this was...another woman? Desmond leaned forward in the doorway.

She stood on the stoop flanked behind by two tethered gondolas. In the clouded light, they looked like wings flaring from her back. She was eighteen, maybe? Twenty? Her clothes were outlandish. A costume? Under it, she was a slim girl, taller than Isa, but not made up of the same punctuating curves.

"Yes?" he asked.

Her round eyes took in his uniform then started roving over the palazzo, confusion building with every blink. "Isn't this—" Her gaze darted down to a scrap of paper clenched in her hand. "I thought this was Thorne & Son, Ltd.? The money exchangers?"

There had never been a son and it had been almost five years since Gilbert Thorne had traded in coins. The first Desmond had always known and the second he'd learned poring over his late uncle's will. Looking for any way out.

"No. I mean, yes. It was, but not now. I'm sorry." The muscles in Desmond's hand tightened as he pushed away from the door still caught in his grip and started moving back.

"But. I—" the young woman began to stammer, oblivious to Desmond's clear intent of ending the conversation. "I was told to come here. To see him." Her eyes were back to searching whatever was written on the paper again. "I was told to see Gilbert Thorne."

Oh. *Oh.*

So, that's how it was. There may have never been a son and there had certainly never been a wife, but receipts and old family gossip had made it clear that the late Thorne had always had a pretty face and fine figure to warm his bed.

Mentally, Desmond groaned. A courtesan didn't care who was paying, just so long as *someone* was. The woman's eyes locked with his.

"No." His tongue stumbled over the two letters of the word, his feet yanking him backwards as his hand fumbled for the door handle. The dragon-faced handle met his fingers with a scraping bite. "Find somewhere else to go," he managed.

She didn't move.

"I'm not interested, thank—good night." There, he had the door by the handle, but before the rest of him could join his feet in retreat, something lit in the young woman's eyes.

Desmond had seen battle dragons before. And whatever was rising inside her was just like the stirring before the blast.

She took a step back, paper crackling in her fist. Her rouged cheeks flushed as if fanned by flame. The layers of silk and lace spinning around her frame fluttered as her next back step almost sent her stumbling off the stoop.

"You think—? You! May the Pale Mercy *spit* on you!"

Without another word she turned and sped away, a white and yellow fairy queen vanishing into a greying world. The first raindrop hit just as Desmond let the door fall shut. For a moment, the building rattle of falling rain was the only sound in the foyer.

"You have seen an actual whore, before, right?"

It was Isa who spoke first.

"And woodcuttings of the Lady of the Scarlet Cord don't count."

Desmond jumped at the sound of Artair's voice right by his ear. *Chords.* The man had not only heard the entire thing, he'd seen it. There was going to be no living this down should they both outlive the Chronicler himself. Desmond fumbled, trying to reset the lock. But Artair's long shadow blocked his sight. The count had one shoulder propped against the door and both arms folded against his chest. His face was the scholastic definition of amused.

"Oh, spit and polish," Desmond growled, giving the door a jiggle that finally set the lock and dislodged Artair.

"I know that girl. I mean, I've seen her before," Isa said. "She's a story dancer with the Troupe Beli. Very definitely *not*—"

Desmond spun around. "Yes, yes, I think the court has determined I'm a raving fool. Thank you for adding to the evidence." Oh, chords, why couldn't he just melt into the marble floor. His eyes met Isadore's. She was looking at him, just like Artair, but her gaze was different. No laughter. There was something hard and searching in her look, something twisted with concern.

...The way he used to look at people. When he cared. When he could afford to care.

"What's wrong with you, Edenry?" Isadore's question pulled Desmond's eyes away from the streets flooding with people and now rainwater. They were heading towards the palace. Finally.

But not before Artair and Isa had drenched the Thorne palazzo in dialogue about the young dancer and her loud wish for Desmond to be—how had she put it—spat upon by Death. Desmond had let out a silent cry of victory when a gondola draped in imperial regalia had finally come for his friend. He had no idea what would come of this meeting of the masters of the world, but Desmond doubted the masses would benefit.

At least he still had the choice of picking his own clothes. He hadn't changed them at all, but if Isa still cared, apparently that wasn't what was on her mind.

"What?" he asked. The coach had splashed through so many starts and stops, Desmond was beginning to feel he was going to be just as seasick as if they'd taken a gondola. He turned to face Isa. Too fast. The contents of his stomach sent up a warning signal that they wouldn't be accepting such behavior again.

"What are you talking about?" he repeated around a hard swallow. Isa's look was as piercing as it had been earlier, but her answer came out soft. Too soft.

"This isn't you."

Desmond eased his shoulders back. His leathers whispered against the velvet plush of the seat. Oh, this was definitely him. Wasn't it? His hand wrapped around his sword hilt as a double comforting reassurance. It didn't help. Feelings, ones he'd been both blocking like a dyke and somehow still drowning in, jabbed at his soul with their ever-churning waves.

Isa leaned forward, closing the distance between them. In the dimming light, he could just catch the shine in her green eyes. "I know people. It's what I do. And I've known you ever since we were all bairns. I know what you've always been. And this isn't it."

If Desmond's eyes hadn't been seared from having watched so many raindrops splatter against the window, he'd have sworn there were tears in Isa's eyes.

This time, his shoulders squirmed against the seat. "By the Dream, Isa, what am I? Enlighten me."

Isadore sank back without a word, her own gaze falling to search the wet world outside the coach.

"You're Desmond Marc Edenry, soldier, son of a soldier," she started, her tone still eerily quiet. "Knighted at eighteen, made captain at twenty-five. You're judgmental, opinionated. By religion, a Sancter. By hobby, a theater critic. Or at least you used to be."

Desmond wasn't sure which of the last two in her list she was referring to in the past tense, but he huffed anyway. "I haven't been inside a sanct in months. The Vawde like to treat anything resembling God like soot on white marble—something to scour away." He made a scrubbing motion in the shadowy air.

"God dwells not in houses made of stone, but inside lives carved of flesh and bone." Isa's reply was a recited one, the words Albidoni Tellers gave to Sancters. Both sects followed the Redeeming God, but each one had strong and differing opinions on how that following was supposed to look. Lounging around teahouses instead of attending services had given Tellers plenty of time to make their side at least sound poetic.

Desmond huffed again. "Well, I've given him plenty to see over the past few years."

At that, Isa's attention still didn't move from the world outside the coach; at least, her sight didn't. But Desmond's trained senses could feel every fiber of her mental focus hone on him. He shifted to the side, drawing his right leg up to balance over his knee, like one final shield between himself and—

"Life is like swearing, did you know that?" Isadore's words were just audible over the toiling of a duo of tower bells somewhere nearby. "In Albidon, we say *chords in flats and sharps*. Flat notes and sharp ones make opposite sounds, yes? They make a song haunting or make it a sweet lullaby—"

"Isa, if you think how we say *chords* is actually swearing, you should spend a day in an army encampment."

Isadore waved him off. "Here, they say *saints and sinners*. Two opposite things. And yet the same thing. Notes of a solo all come from one instrument and what a man turns out to be is still the embodiment of that one life.

"I know this isn't what you planned." Her eyes caught his now. "But life, it doesn't look like we expected it to. For better or for worse"—the bells were overhead now reaching the culmination of their song—"life is both good and bad. Not just one or the other."

Desmond felt the catch of her gaze give a tug and at the second bell's answer to the first's call to crescendo, the raging flood inside him broke free. "At least I would like the privilege of *choosing* my bad," he started, the words spilling out with nothing to stop them now. "What? You think I used to walk through the world thinking it was all sunshine and Rising Day roses?" His hand smacked the seat beside him.

"I *know* the world's a mountain-high pile of manure." He hit the seat again, this time with fingers curled in a fist. "That's why I chose a soldier's life, to protect the innocent from it. But this?" The laugh he let out was so heavy with bitterness, he could taste it on his tongue. "I feel nothing for the cause of this war. In fact, I would say we're probably on the wrong side of it. I—"

"If a master gives you a set of notes, and to them you can add no more, and take away no less, what's the one thing you can do?"

Desmond didn't answer.

"You can choose the key, Edenry. You can choose the mood, the pace. There is always a way to make a choice." Her voice sounded suddenly hard at that, like something different had come to her mind. "Did you know," she said, "that in this city they tie you to a pyre and set you aflame just for even thinking differently than the matriarchs tell you? *Choice* is precious."

But before Desmond could reply or even ingest her words, Isa's hand was around the lapel of his vest, her other hand pushing the coach door open. She yanked him forward. "Look," she whispered.

Anyone else grabbing him like that would have quickly found their brain matter decorated with their teeth, but this close again to Isa's perfume was paralyzing. And so was the sight that met Desmond's eyes.

Before them sprawled his destination. The Palace Imperial with its great gate made not of gold, but carved bar by bar from bone. Human or animal, no one knew. And those who did were only silent sentries now.

But beyond the palace, gilding the stone in a gold of its own, piercing like an explosion through windows and gaps in turrets, was the setting sun. It had never seemed so large. So harsh and potent in its light.

"You can look east or you can look west." Isa's voice was at Desmond's ear, her words rushing over each other like a stream eager to join a greater river. "It's all the same sky and we live under it. But one side has rain, and the other has a sunset. Where will you put your eyes? I know what I said about money, Des—"

Isa's hand fell away as she pulled back into the coach. Without looking back at him, she started tugging on her gloves, stretching them out finger by finger. "But choose for yourself what weapon you use tonight. I know you." She repeated the phrase before wiggling her last pinky. "You're Desmond Marc Edenry. I may know people, but you see them." She hesitated a heartbeat. "You *see*, and you care. Be that person. Driver!"

The coach lurched forward at the command, giving Desmond no choice but to scramble the rest of the way out of his seat. His feet hit the cobbles hard. "Rhym," he growled through the jar that raced from his soles all the way to his jaw. But the coach was gone. Isadore off to the ship that would take her God knew where.

"Welcome, citizens of the Masque and all followers of our merciful Mother!" The voice yanked Desmond's attention from the disappearing coach and to his immediate surroundings. He wasn't the only one standing before the palace gates. With a heavy creak accompanied by a blare of trumpets, they swung open.

That had been the plan on how Desmond would get to the fourth prince. On the night of the Masque's most religious holiday, a day when all crime and all sin went overlooked, the home of the imperial family was open to any and all. Desmond didn't understand why on a night like this the Drakes thought themselves safe with the rabble of the city unleashed within their walls, but maybe their own sins were a black shield so much worse. He'd believe that.

Desmond slid up beside an elderly woman and started walking in step with the blossoming crowd. As he passed a second level of gates about forty paces in, Desmond noticed the bone bars were wrapped in ribbons of scarlet silk. One piece trailed onto the ground like—

A shudder ran through him. At its force, the contents of his stomach threatened him harder than they ever had in the coach.

Death. Death. The master of this city, the snuffer of lives, so many of them through Desmond's very own hand. With a sidestep, he veered off the path and buckled to his knees behind a tall tree. It loomed over him, shivering its white blooms in the quiet breeze.

"Where will you set your eyes?" Isadore's words whispered in the back of his mind. Pulling his gaze up, Desmond looked for the sun, desperately, like a drowning man thrashing for the surface. But it was gone now; only one final horizontal gleam flickered beneath a series of banners.

The opposite of rain was sunlight. White could not be more different than black. All things had opposites.

And so did death. It had to. Wrapping a trembling hand around a branch, he heaved himself back to his feet. Petals fell off into his palm as he pulled his hand away. He looked at them. It was spring. He'd barely noticed the seasons for years, only feeling the blaze of summer as it had baked him inside his armor and the frosty chill of winter as it bit through a tent at night. He drew in a breath of the petals' scent. Strong and wild like lemons. Spring brought—

The thing Desmond had seen in the periwinkle eyes of that young dancer on the palazzo stoop: raw and raging, but real—

Life.

SEVEN

LAUDILAS

The world was a riot: of people, of color...of crime. Laudilas had seen two murders so far. The first had been right outside his room in the Rex and Rod. Just as the nearest tower bells had struck six, the shouting had started, followed by a grunt, then a thump. Laude had been forced to step over the body on his way out. Nobody looked like they'd be bothering to clear it away anytime soon.

The second had been a few minutes ago. Laude was in the westernmost garden of the Imperial Palace now, the one lit by the intermittent flame of caged firebirds and lined with spindly cypress trees. Two rival members of the Senate had just settled what looked like a decades-old quarrel by both succumbing to the poison they'd intended for the other.

"Moon-mad lunatics," Laude muttered loud enough for at least a dozen people to hear as he pushed his way out of the garden. But those around him were more interested in seeing if the now late senators' sons would start dueling to the death or making peace. The raucous, off-kilter mood of the crowd all but screamed which one they were hoping for.

Laude forced his throat to swallow, but his mouth was as dry as if one of the firebirds had breathed straight into him. He swiped a hand under the nearest fountain, scooping the water down in one hard gulp.

This was the third garden he had tried in his search for Prince Luca. For a young man who his brother claimed wasn't a recluse, he was proving as hard to find as decency and sanity tonight.

Settling himself on the fountain's edge, Laude began tracing the stonework with a wet finger. "If tonight was tonight and I felt out of sorts even on a good day, where would I be?" The stone didn't answer. But Laude knew exactly where he'd be, whole-bodied or frail. He'd be drunk.

The only information Benerict had further supplied about the prince was that he was a scholar—or at least he had been some years ago before his last health upset. If the young man was still bookishly inclined, where—

"Oh, chords, a library," Laude groaned. He pushed to his feet. As he did, a jutting lip of stonework caught at the silk of his long surcoat. Maybe it hadn't cared to answer his questions, but apparently the fountain wasn't bored with him just yet. He snatched the silver-stitched hem away.

He should have thought of this earlier. Warriors like his brother found refuge behind their armor. Drunkards, like people claimed he was, found their protection from the world inside glass bottles. So, scholars would hide within walls and stacks of books. "Why don't I just ask a guard to take me down to a dungeon and string me up by my thumbs? It'd be less painful and more pleasant company." He let out a hiss between his teeth.

In Albidon, people knew exactly where libraries were, even if they were like him and had never darkened the door of one. But here, Laudilas might as well have been asking where he could join a service celebrating the resurrection of the Redeeming God.

He knew the palace grounds doubtless had multiple enclaves for books. The chances that he'd hit on the right one first time around were not odds he'd put any silver on, but if he could just at least get in the right company... Where people thought with words and not—

The sharp, sudden scent of something burning cut through his senses. He'd moved on from the fountain and was making his way through a series of interconnecting balconies. Coming from the sprawling courtyard at the heart of the central palace were the sounds of lutes and violins playing a fast-paced melody. There'd be dancing there. Laude made a mental note of the courtyard's location. As soon as this book business was over, he would need a drink and a lovely maid to dance with.

The smell came again. His nose jerked his eyes to the narrow piazza directly below him. There was no music there, but a crowd of white-robed women were gathered. They all stood in a semicircle around a pyre that had just been lit. One stepped forward, breaking the curve, and began to chant in a language Laude could only catch a word or two of. The flames leapt higher as the woman's arms raised into the air then plunged down to grasp the wet earth.

A scream ripped through the air. Laude's long legs pulled him into a run before his mind had even issued the command. Three balconies and a long set of stairs later, he finally made it back to solid ground.

"By the six sunken cities, what was *that*?" There was a difference between settling old scores or making off with your best mate's sweetheart for a night, but there had been *people* on that pyre. Real, living ones. People who didn't look like they'd been given a fighting chance. Laude was an actor; he knew when a scream was faked and when it was not. A shiver ran through him.

"You mean over there?" A voice rumbled down at Laudilas from at least two inches above his head. A mountain made of flesh and bone stood in front of him, blocking his path. The man had arms probably the exact measurements of Laude's own waist. He grunted. "Mediatrix herself, come to sacrifice the faithless to the Mother." Dark eyes looked Laude up and down like a bear browsing a meat market. The man sniffed. "First time?"

The faithless? Laude was pretty sure he fit in that category. Probably top of the list since his faith wasn't in anything except maybe his brother's talent at ruining his life.

"Mediatrix?" he asked. The question spilled out of him even though he didn't really expect the man to answer. *Mediatrix.* The title sounded familiar.

Officially, House Drake recognized the new, nonroyal government of Albidon. But over the years Benerict had still wined and dined every prince and imperial concubine he could. Anything to curry favors. *The wind always shifts, little brother. Remember that. Someday, it will shift.*

So, Laude had grown up knowing all the names and faces of the Masque's ruling political elite. But tonight wasn't about politics. *Mediatrix...*

Oh...

Memory hit him just as the man started to speak again. "The link between life and death, the one who speaks to the Red Lady on man's behalf."

Wasn't that Death's job? To speak for man before the Darkness? Wait, that wasn't what the mountain-man had said. Chords. This intercessory dance was beginning to sound more like a gossip chain than a religion.

But he remembered now. The mediatrix was a mind molder. Unlike Laude's gift of illusion, mind molders actually did things, the stronger the molder, the more powerful their influence over a man's thoughts...and will.

Images from the past flooded his mind as the smell of choked-out life still lingered even down here. He had been seventeen when his brother had taken him to the Masque on one of his visits. Laude had spent most of the trip trying to woo the heart of a young contessa he'd met on the voyage over. But he did remember being dragged to some opulent affair held out in the open at the city's center. Everything had been washed in red and snow white.

As a youth, he had thought all the colors were romantic, but looking back now, he'd been at the induction of the new mediatrix. She had only been fifteen, and for the first time in two centuries, she had been a Drake. The imperial house now ruled in both the mortal and immortal affairs of their subjects.

Another image flashed through his mind's eye. Of another young person that day; this one had been robed all in red just like the new mediatrix except he hadn't been waving to an adoring crowd. He'd been laid out on a velvet-draped bier like an offering, displayed for all to see. The boy's face had been pale as the moon, despite his bright garb, and almost as shadowed-pocked.

"She's so powerful because her twin is giving his life to her," someone in the crowd had said.

"The Mother will take him gently, then? Will she? He looks ready for her."

The question had been from a little child in the crowd. Laude had to agree with the child. The boy even now in memory had looked broken and wrong.

He grabbed the man by both trunk-sized arms. "The Mediatrix, she's the twin of Prince Luca? Hmm?"

Oh, chords. Benerict wanted him to take a book from that poor thing?

If that had been the crowd's opinion of the young prince back then, an afflicted sacrifice increasing the power of their hope—one of their hopes—between heaven and hell, what did the sacrifice think of it? Especially now that he'd apparently decided he wasn't interested in stepping into Death's arms quite so young.

Either he was as radical as those women in that piazza—or—

The man brushed Laude away like a hurricane would dislodge a feather. But his tone was suddenly intense, his dark eyes boring into Laude's. "What do you want with His Highness?"

"Talk books?" Laude heard his voice come out in a squeak. *Chords.* At least it made him sound less threatening. The man certainly looked like he would more than threaten anything or anyone who crossed the prince in question. Maybe some radical devotee.

One heartbeat. Two.

"That way." The man pointed a thick finger towards the sound of the music Laudilas had heard earlier. "You'll find what you want that way." And then he was gone.

Laude let out a whistle. The man had left with no sound and no trace. Even a spy extraordinaire like Isadore Rhym would have been impressed.

As he followed the music, chasing it like a siren's call, Laude found himself passing through the great doors of the central palace and entering a vast foyer splayed open on all sides like an amphitheater. The sudden passage from outdoors to indoors then out again was doubtless some subliminal mind game by the Drakes. But what it was, Laude had no idea.

He had never been in this building before where the heart of an empire thrummed with life and dealt out death. He'd only ever skirted around in the smaller side palaces with Benerict, like a beggar seeking for castoff crumbs.

Columns, five times the height of most men, stood guard on all four sides. As he stepped between two of the nearest columns, he glanced up. Carved faces looked down at him, faces of creatures Laude had never seen. They were either from the most ancient history or the imagination of very bored men.

Here, inside the palace's open face, the world seemed even more of a riot. But this chaos was different. There was a bizarre, fevered order to it, as if people's eyes weren't focused on what they could get out of the freedom the night offered. It was what they could get out of the people around them that had everyone's attention.

And most eyes were on one man in particular.

"People of Vawdawr! It's time we throw off the yoke of those who rule over us in our Mother's name. They claim to know her heart, but how do we know this? Their laws they say are for our own good, like the guidance of our own blessed mothers, but the Mediatrix and her Maidens do not wed nor bear children. How can they know what it's like? How can they understand the most precious relationship between mother and child?"

Prince Amadeo. The third of the Imperator's sons. The brawny but eloquent man stood at the foot of a marble statue that boasted of little clothing and even less hair. Ever since Laude could remember, Amadeo had been a troublemaker. First in stealing Laude's shoes when they'd been boys and now, for the past half a decade, the princeling had been trying to steal his father's youngest concubine and his throne.

The role of imperator didn't pass from eldest to eldest. It was won like everything the Drakes possessed. By conquest. Amadeo had always proven himself the strongest son, but he had a weakness. Something normal people would call good sense. The man wanted to marry.

But according to laws dictated from some mediatrix now dead and moldering in the ground, the imperators of the Masque could not wed, but were commanded to have as many women as their hearts desired, every generation blessed with an abundance of Drakes coming into this world.

"They say my love is a sin, but I say it is a true and right thing. Why do we let them run our mortal lives? Let the Red Seat rule in all things heavenly and let us rule in all things here below!"

A raucous cheer went up from the fifty or so people gathered. Laude moved on. The music, not politics, was calling him.

The first time he had seen the courtyard and heard its music had been from above. From up there, the whole place had seemed lit as with the sun itself. Now underneath the bright, spinning lights that dangled down from unseen wires, Laude found himself caught in the swirling dance of scores if not hundreds of people.

This close to the music, he could discern each instrument. The silver flutes, the whistles with their wild, untamed trills, the soft thrum of lute strings. And racing over them all was the heavy sound of strings: cello, violin, viola—chords, was that a Sagar?

Sagar violins were rare, invented and crafted by an Albidoni master over a century ago. They had one or two extra strings adding to the instrument's range, making its sound unique and distinct.

And that's when he saw him. He had spotted the Sagar too, piercing grey eyes fixed like an archer on a target. Except it wasn't his target. It wasn't Laude's either.

Sweeping between two velvet-clad women, one slim as a willow, the other round as a barrel and almost as short, Laude moved dance step by dance step towards the sidelines. He bowed to both of his partners, then reaching out a hand, tapped the violin-enamored man on the shoulder. "Care to dance?"

Desmond Edenry whirled, but not in any rhythm but a deadly one. His eyes blinked once then twice before focusing on something that was unfortunately human and not made of wood and strings. He scowled, shaking his head, brows bent in something between confusion and consternation.

Laude flashed his best smile. "Excellent then." He puffed out a breath. "You're entirely too male and too short for my tastes anyway. Come, we need to talk."

"Too short—*what?*"

Laude didn't turn back to see if the Falcon captain was following him. A part of him wasn't even sure this was a good idea. *Do you invite a rival gang to approve of your plans before you break into a countinghouse? The one that has the same treasure they're after?*

But Laudilas was desperate and not for the reasons he expected to be tonight. What he'd seen those women do—a shudder ran down his spine as he rounded a narrow corridor and stepped into another foyer. This one was small and boasted of a heavy roof carved from stone so polished it cast a slight gleam in the dim light. He needed to see, to talk to someone from the land of sanity. And if any man was sane, it was Desmond Edenry.

"If you think you're going to wheedle me into some dark corner, slit my throat, then take the diary, I haven't got it." Desmond's voice came from directly behind him. But it didn't carry with it the cadence of moving footsteps. The man had stopped and wouldn't be going any farther, not without more information. And maybe not even with that.

Laude turned. "What? You haven't got a throat?" Desmond stood at the bottom of the trio of stairs Laude had just climbed, one hand wrapped around his sword hilt and the other resting suspiciously behind his back. *I wager if you turn him upside down and give him a good shake, enough pointy metal would fall out to outfit a regiment.*

"Libraries," Laude said, eager to cover up his miserable joke. "We'll find the prince in one of those. That's the place." If he had Desmond to either race in front of or trail behind, he didn't care. The captain had always been a focused man and Laude *needed* focus. There had to be nigh a thousand torches lit tonight sparking their smoke over ten thousand perfumed revelers, but only one scent still lingered in his—

"Already looked in all—" Desmond interrupted his thoughts; the man was counting off on his fingers but stopped when he ran out at five. His other hand didn't move from his sword hilt. "Six of them. Nothing and no one there."

Laude wasn't sure if Desmond meant absolutely no one or just no one helpful. The only thing in the foyer was yet another set of stairs. These reached sprawling horizontal fingers up and up until they vanished in a sudden bend. Laude dropped down onto the bottom step. "So." He slapped a hand against the tread. The metal of his rings kissed the marble with a clink. "His Highness remains a mystery."

Why had the mountain-man sent him here, though? *You'll find what you want that way.* Well, he had found Desmond. But that wasn't what he'd assumed the man thought he wanted... They had been talking about the prince, not someone else who was looking for him.

Laude cut into his own musings this time. "But when we do find him, what do you plan to do?" he asked. One of Desmond's eyebrows cocked up like a drawn bowstring. Laude let out a deep sigh. "Humor me."

"Hmm." With some deliberate thought, Desmond propped one foot onto the step in front of him and let his hand fall from his sword hilt to drape over his knee, then said, "Bribing; you?"

Laude shrugged. "Charming."

"And if all else fails?"

It took Laude only a split heartbeat to know the answer. "Stealing."

"I'd say all else was failing."

"We haven't found him yet."

Desmond just nodded as if that proved his point. Seeing the screwed-up expression Laude didn't even try to hide, he continued. "It's the diary we're both trying to take home to Mama, right? A book doesn't have legs; it can't have gone off on holiday all the way to Uroshii Under the Moon already. Forget this prince. Find the book."

Laude wasn't sure if he should address the idea that the captain saw this whole venture as something akin to taking a girl home for the lady of the house's approval or the fact his last two sentences had begun with commanding verbs or—

"His Highness doesn't have legs either, ones that hold him up anyway," he put in instead, standing to his own feet. "So, yes, I doubt he and his new treasure are off in the White City."

In the circular foyer, the two men stood, facing each other. The Knight doing his duty to a friend with a little undercurrent of antimonarchist sentiment for added incentive. And there was him. The Brother, the son of kings and queens long dead, trying to retrieve something that had once belonged to one of them.

He wondered if Queen Adile would thank him. Or were the rebels right? That the Albidoni royal family had descended so far from what their forebears intended that the old queen would side with the Unmaker and his lot without a second thought.

There was only one way to find out. He had to get the diary. It might just be legacy, but it also contained the foundational thoughts of that legacy. For once, he was just sober enough to be interested.

"So," he said, folding his arms across his chest. "What are we? Members of a *banda di strada* out for our next hit? Or are we going to play rival master criminals and pull off a heist, one of us ends up gutted in the canal for the grand finale?"

Desmond cleared the distance between them in surprisingly quick strides for a man who spent so much time atop a horse. "I don't care which role you want to play, de Glas. Whatever costume and props you want to use. No one is ending up with so much as a bump on the knee. Understand? If you think you're going home with some fantastic tale of how we dueled with razor-sharp blades across rooftops for this thing, you *aren't*."

In the patterned light dancing on the stone walls, Laude could see a strange, determined heat in Desmond's pale eyes. The man was mad, furious even about something. But it wasn't directed at him... Desmond blinked and the look was gone.

"Besides, if we did, you wouldn't be the one going home, still with breath in your lungs for speaking, anyway," he added almost as an afterthought. "Whoever gets it first, gets it. Simple as that. No blood, no bodies.

"Now, I was going to suggest trying the prince's bedchamber. Isa told me where it was." Then without anything as formal as an invitation or a *get your backside over here*, the captain turned on his heel and started for the step Laude had just vacated.

"Bedchamber?" Now it was Laude's turn to be both astounded and give chase. He caught up with Desmond just as the staircase took its sharp turn to the left.

"Hm, that's right."

Laude's head gave a shake, his legs fumbling to match the movement with the forward pace of walking. "Do I want to know how she knows so much about bedrooms?" he muttered.

Desmond cast him a sideways glance. "Not for the same reasons as half this city."

"Give me your vote this session in the Senate and we will make a better city together!" Amadeo's voice came back into earshot as the two cleared a corridor and found themselves looking down over the crowd still assembled in the open foyer Laude had passed through earlier.

"Doesn't he know his half-sister makes a barbecue out of people who say things like that?" Laude's words came out in a whisper. He hadn't meant for them to come out at all. That young woman with her hands dug deep into the living earth probably had eyes and ears everywhere. Almost subconsciously, he cast a glance up at the carved faces still looking down from their colonnade perches.

"I thought witches who lived in rock candy houses did that?"

Laude swiveled full-bodied around on Desmond. The man just shrugged. There was levity in his dry smirk, but none in his eyes.

When Desmond finally spoke, it was in a quiet, but icy undertone. "I know what you mean; Isa told me."

"Well, I don't care what Lady Rhym said, I know what I *saw*," Laude spat.

Both men stood facing each other again for a moment, gripped in a silent tug of war. There was that heat again in the captain's eyes. Around them the world pulsed, loud and red. Instinctively, Laude reached inside of himself, grasping for answers. But his trained senses, those of both actor and soldier, could give only a single reply.

One voice cannot silence the thunder and a lone white flag will only turn as red as the flood of blood it tries to staunch. One person, even two, could do nothing for whatever eldritch hands held this city together while its claws tore it apart. Not now. Not today.

It seemed Desmond had come to the same conclusion. The knight was moving again, away from the sounds and towards a long hallway rendered wall-to-wall in fantastical paintings. When it ended, Desmond wordlessly veered into another hallway, this one narrower than the one before but just as paint-splattered with faces and creatures.

They were almost to the end of a third hallway before Laude realized what Desmond had been doing. The paintings were telling a story and he was following it, looking for a certain—

Without warning, both the hall and the captain's footsteps came to an abrupt stop. A set of double doors stood in their way. Tangling around and over the frame of both doors, obvious even in the dim torchlight, was the image of two dragons locked in battle. One white. One red.

"Here we are."

There was no guard in front of the double doors. In fact, light could be seen coming through a small crack where their edges almost, but didn't quite meet. It was inviting. Like a beckoning finger and a wink from a rascal sibling just before a trick. The hairs on the back of Laude's neck prickled in warning. But Desmond already had a hand around one handle, easing the door open without so much as a creak.

In contrast to the hall, the room that met their eyes was as bright as daylight. In every corner of the oddly angled room, tall candelabras cast warm, yellow light over—

Books. Hundreds of them. Probably thousands. Laude let out a silent groan as he followed Desmond into the room. Spliced between windows and free-standing like sentries, were over a dozen bookshelves. The spines of the books glinted in fresh reds, dark greens, peeling browns, and unassuming blacks, some in color-coded order, some in order of height, and many in no order at all.

"There's no one here," Desmond said, stopping suddenly less than halfway into the chamber. Laude didn't bother to ask him how he could tell. Falcons weren't considered the best warriors east of the Feathered Wastes for no good reason.

"So, we look?"

Desmond turned to a case shorter than the rest that held scrolls poking out from circular slots. Laude watched as he traced a finger over the edge of one without actually touching the ragged parchment.

"If you can." There was a smirking edge to the captain's voice, a challenge, one that mixed about as well as water and oil with the prickling sensation still reverberating through Laude's nerves.

He pushed past the scroll case. "Oh, don't get your sword in a twist," he muttered to Desmond's back. "I know how to read."

He glanced down at his feet. There was no sound as the soles of his boots clicked by. *Disappointing.*

The carpet beneath him was thick, thicker than most he'd seen in his life. Meant to silence the sound. He glanced up at the open windows. They too were framed by thick curtains, drawn back for now, but with cords that had the look of little use.

It was like the inhabitant of this room needed dark and quiet more often than not. So why was everything so bright tonight? It was as if the entire place had been set up for someone else... A flash of memory of the mountain-man and his strange directions sent the raw sensation still thrumming through Laude up another notch. He dove for the shadows deeper in the room.

Despite the multi-angled features of the chamber's outer ring, it had looked normal, like something that could be found in a university or the home of any number of particularly boring people. But further in, things changed.

It was a bedroom, true enough. Lady Rhym hadn't gotten that wrong. There was a canopied bed, miscellaneous furniture, and even a large bathtub built into the wall of a rounded corner. Everything looked comfortable and used. But comfortable in the sense that things had been made for the ease of other people, not necessarily the occupant of the room.

The bed was an odd width. The canopy looming over it had the size of something that had once housed a much larger mattress but had been robbed of its glory for something narrower. Whoever rested in that bed wouldn't tumble out but could still be tended to from both sides. Tonight, it was empty of both occupant—and any books—old or newly acquired.

Laude sniffed. This close to the more personal life of the fourth prince imperial smelled less like books and over lit candles and more like—he drew in another breath, then stifled it before it could release in full. He didn't even bother looking at the large dressing table opposite the bed. The smells told him there would be only jars and bottles there, and not the kind a young man used to woo the ladies.

His eyes kept moving. Some people read while soaking in the tub—so he'd been told. But all his perusal of the prince's curved tub told him that someone had twisted it into a convenience for others as well. There was a frame inside that looked like it was meant to support a body whether in part or in full and a step wide enough for comfortable kneeling had also been carved into the side of the tub. Laude's shoulders shivered at the depressing image the whole thing conjured. He'd have to remember it if he ever needed to jerk up a good tear while on stage.

Where is the chords-blasted diary of great-great-somewhere-back-there grandmama, though...

If the prince had only acquired the diary this morning, a gambler's chances were that he had not shelved it yet, so it should be here with his more personal effects. The faint shuffling sounds coming from behind told him Desmond was still in the outer part of the chamber, looking shelf by shelf.

Method versus mayhem, that's what we are.

A tapestry caught his eye. It hung opposite the tub in fading threads like the characters stitched there had spent years trying to hide their eyes from the room's living occupant and his sad life. But one corner was even more worn. It was a small spot. About the size of a hand. Laude made for it.

His palm and fingers wrapped over the spot, fitting it like a tailor-made glove. He started to pull the cloth back. The door under the tapestry swung open with a creak as if it had been pulled. Not pushed...

Laude jumped back.

Desmond might have felt no one in the prince's chambers when they entered, but *something* wasn't right.

"You there!"

The silence of two men in the middle of a heist turned, in a split heartbeat, to the clank and clamor of three well-armed guards. The trio stood in the middle of the now fully open double doors. One with his sword drawn and the other two with gleaming pikes lowered for action.

Laude didn't move, but his eyes darted, scraping across every visible inch of the room. Desmond was nowhere to be seen. He could step forward, throw himself into the room behind the tapestry and shut its door. He could be out a window—the room had to have a window—and gone before these over-armored, over-fed guards could catch him.

But what had pulled that door open? What, or rather, *who* was on the other side? The prickles chasing up and down Laude's spine were now strong enough to lift hair even as long as his.

The guard with the sword sashayed into the room. "Well, well, what do we have here?"

How original, Laude heard the one small part of his brain that wasn't panicking mutter. The guards. Or the door. Or—

"Well, there you are." Laude's arms crossed over his chest and his lungs drew in a deep breath, then let it flare out slowly, deliberately. He knew the poses. He knew the tone. The ones only royal blood made possible. That ability to look in and expect total control of a situation—even if your insides were strongly wishing you were still two with a nappy around your waist to catch what your bowels really wanted to do. "I've been waiting for His Highness for the past half hour. Which one of you miserable lugs failed to let him know? Hmm?"

The guard with the sword blinked as Laude cleared the distance between them. Mentally, he cursed again the thick carpet and his silenced footfalls. The man opened his mouth, then shut it, but not in time to keep the expelled scent of too much wine and maybe something stronger from slipping into the air.

"You? Who—" The words came out in a slur as the guard shook his head as if trying to reconnect the thoughts that were getting cut off by too much liquid.

"They're stealing."

Laude felt his bravado snap like a rotten saddle strap. *Chords.*

Stepping from behind the tapestry was the mountain-man, his broad frame filling the corner of Laude's vision, and his calm, low voice flooding the rest of him with the raw thumping of his heart.

"Huh? *They?* There's just this one. Yeah?" The guards with the pikes had descended into the chamber as well. Laude found himself reaching a protective hand up to his throat as his breath involuntarily jerked down in a hard swallow. The one talking was waving his pike in Laude's direction, the candelabras casting their light a little too encouragingly against its shiny spearhead.

"He means me." Desmond appeared around the corner of a bookshelf, hands by his sides, an innocent look on his face as he cast a glance at Laude.

Where in the name of nightmares have you been? Laude wanted to hiss. But the pike was still aimed in his direction.

The pike-pointing guard looked at Desmond with all the interest of mud to rain. "So," he drawled, his own voice sounding weighed down by one glass of wine too many. "You tried to steal from His Highness too, did you?"

Desmond sighed, settling himself back against the wall of the bookshelf, hands still in view. Everything about him was casual, as if he stole things every day and got caught every other. Laude watched him with one eye while keeping the other's sight firmly fixed on the mountain-man.

With silent ease, Desmond placed one foot slightly in front of the other. Laude sensed the mountain-man tense. Only someone who knew the deep secrets of steel dancing would know what the Falcon captain was actually doing. Laude took one deliberate step forward. If Desmond and this man made of muscle and apparently a little too much knowledge of the Albidoni art of sword fighting were about to lock onto each other like male dogs, he didn't want to be the bone in between.

But Desmond just sighed again. "No," he said, his voice carrying an edge that teetered the fine line between laughter and tired tears. "But I've been thinking about it a lot. That's not the same thing, no?"

The first guard slammed his sword into its sheath, thought apparently rising over the flood of wine just enough to take command of the situation again.

"This is La Notte, Merced." He flipped his hands, palms out towards the mountain-man. "Nothing I can do if they decided to make off with the whole lot of this." He waved one hand over the vicinity of the entire chamber.

"I think that's for His Highness to decide."

Merced... That wasn't a surname, it was a title. From Ansyra? Laude couldn't place the word. But the mountain-man's next words were as iron-hard as his massive shoulders looked.

"His Highness will see them *now*."

Laude's eyes locked with Desmond's. The man's brow was furrowed, hand back to his sword, but it didn't look like he intended to draw it. His fingers were twisting around the falcon-headed hilt as if the movement was somehow comforting.

The Merced turned to them both. His next words were the same as his last, but the hairs on Laude's neck didn't prickle this time.

Instead, as he and Desmond were pushed between the guards and forced through the door, past the two dragons still locked in paint and fight, he had the eerie, distinct feeling of being a marionette on strings. Strings being pulled by someone who'd planned this too well...or for too long.

EIGHT

DESMOND

The kitchens.

Well, I didn't see that coming.

Desmond leaned back against a long wooden table, its top dusted with swirls of brown and white sugar. He let his hands curl around the table's edge. The heels of his palms stuck to the mess almost instantly, but it kept his hands in view of his captors.

The long walk from the prince's chambers three stories down to the kitchens seemed to have sobered them a little. Or maybe it was the near-presence of royalty. *Imperial royalty.* That had to be like apples that weren't just rotten. They were worm-riddled rotten.

Desmond glanced at Laudilas. The young de Glas stood across from him, slim frame illuminated by a fire burning in the mouth of a large, open-faced oven. He was picking at the high-low hem of his long doublet, his raven eyebrows puckered like a badly stitched wound. He was nervous.

Desmond's own heart gave a few fast kicks against the wall of his chest. One step after another. That's how life was lived, or so he'd been told. But no one had said how much energy it took to walk through war, through gold...through games. Chords, he was tired. Parts of him that he hadn't before paid much mind gave a throbbing ache as the extra blood surged through his system.

His eyes wandered from Laudilas to his surroundings. This kitchen was the last one, only walled on three sides. The fourth wall was the world. There was no sun blazing brave against a stormy sky now. Not a single stitch of light threaded through the thick shroud of darkness. It had to be close to midnight.

Desmond let his eyes squeeze shut. Without the steady rhythm of his plan to guide his mind, Isadore's words came flooding back in.

Choose for yourself what weapon you will use.

He'd tried that. The prince's bedchamber should have been an easy steal. A small note saying what account the young man could draw out whatever amount he wanted would have taken the book's place. But now the note was still in Desmond's inner pocket. The parchment crinkled slightly as he flexed his shoulders and arms, sending energy down into his hands to dig against the wood even harder.

He'd seen the judgment in Laudilas' glare as they'd left the room. There hadn't been so much as a rat within three chambers when they'd entered, he'd swear his life on that. But something had changed just before the guards had come. *Should have called for a retreat.*

His eyes flew open. In all the battles he had fought, all the skirmishes, all the midnight raids, he'd learned one thing—everything, even stalemates like this had come to, were never really a dead draw. One side always lost more than the other, even if by a hair's breadth. And Laudilas, blundering dolt that he was, was still the opposition in this mission, not one of his men to be shoved out of the way of a flying arrow.

—Or is this son of an empire the opposition now?

"You." The hulking man who had turned them in—while simultaneously turning Laudilas' face almost as white as his hair—stepped into view. He beckoned with one finger. Just one single movement.

The Merced. It was a name Ansyrans gave to only one man in a generation. Their bravest, most feared warrior. But such a man served no one, not even an imperial prince. Not willingly, anyway.

As Desmond stepped past the man and out into the open night with Laudilas trotting just behind him, he swept his gaze over every inch of exposed skin on the man's neck and corded arms.

There. A *styx* brand just below his left ear. So, a convicted murderer then, or at least someone who'd killed the wrong Vawde. Someone now in the service of an imperial Vawde.

Definitely a story there.

The square courtyard they stepped into was braced on all four sides by a low wall made up of the same bricks that now paved the ground beneath their feet. Even the bubbling fountain moored to the center of the courtyard had been built mostly from the same reddish bricks.

"Bow." Laudilas' voice hissed in his ear.

Desmond cut him a glance. Despite himself, his lips twitched up in response to an irreverent chuckle starting inside him. That was the thing about royalty. Each one had someone else even they bowed to.

Laudilas' hiss turned to a jab in the ribs as his long hair swept against Desmond's sleeve with the downward tip of his head.

Desmond scanned the courtyard. If he was going to be bobbing like a pelican on a beach, he'd like to at least be doing it in the right direction. *There.* Servants dressed in red. Guards in gold. But only one figure caught his vision, clad in garments darker than the night, as if in defiance of the vast expanse of sky that flanked him. As Desmond dipped his head, a memory flooded his mind along with a rush of blood.

Albidonis' most fervent desire may have been freedom, but their most particular talent was gossip. And since they no longer had a proper royal family of their own to tattle and surmise about, other nations' ruling houses had filled the bill.

He remembered being in a teahouse in Prevecost five years ago, curled over a particularly spicy cup of ginger tea while a group of physicians loudly debated the case of the Imperator's invalid son.

It's the most singular case I've ever heard of. It's like being a prisoner in your own body. He can't move anymore. He can't even speak.

I'd try—

Desmond didn't remember all the remedies and cures that had been debated that day. But one thing he did recall—

They'd never listen to us. They're sticking to the old ways. They'll kill him that way. On my life, they will.

But apparently, they hadn't killed him.

Tonight, Luca Drake sat length-wise on a low stem-wall, his back resting against a trellis dripping with yellow roses. Unlike almost everyone else Desmond had seen that evening, the prince wore his clothes in black gilded with golden threads. The wide sleeves of his long doublet draped down over the wall, almost licking at the floor.

The young man looked like a playboy scholar in repose, his long legs stretched out before him, crossed lazily at the ankles. There was a book in the prince's lap, but as he straightened from his bow, Desmond could tell it was upside down.

Their eyes met.

You see *people.* Isadore's voice. Desmond yanked his gaze away.

"So." Without prelude or warning, the prince's voice hit the air, soft but with a rumble like distant thunder. It had a deeper tone than seemed to suit his face, but there was no mistaking who was in charge now. One hand rested atop the book in his lap, but with the other, the young royal reached inside his doublet and pulled out another smaller book, its back cover engraved with a small nightingale. He held it up. "Looking for this?"

Desmond felt Laudilas step even closer, their shoulders bumping. *One more inch and the boy's going to think we came joined at the hip.*

No blood. No bodies. That's what he'd promised. To Laudilas, to himself. Some men were born with wisdom, but life eventually brought knowledge to all. And life had made certain Desmond knew exactly what the Drakes were capable of. A shiver of apprehension blazed through him like lightning answering the prince's thunder. There was only one way to know how deep it would strike.

Look at him, a voice whispered.

See *him*, called another.

To look and to see were two things separated by a vast gulf. The first only required eyes. The second, your heart. Isa was right. Desmond had seen once, perhaps so deeply, his own people would call him a wishwalker, a loreborn connected to the thrumming heartbeat of the world itself. But when *looking* only took in the red spray of innocent blood again and again, *seeing* had become an agony he could no longer bear.

Still, he forced his eyes back up. To study, he told himself, to strategize, nothing more.

"Your Most Imperial Highness. Please forgive this egregious intrusion upon your time. If you would grant me only a moment to explain—"

Besides, de Glas is talking. How deeply do I want that *seared into my memory.*

Laudilas had stepped away from Desmond, but sideways. He hadn't actually moved forward. He was bowing again. But this was a player's bow, one meant for the stage. The man hadn't been lying when he said he could charm.

Can I bribe? Besides the trio of guards who had seemed more than happy to just let them walk away with any of the prince's belongings, there were only servants around. As his eyes scanned the shadows, Desmond saw no one waiting to swing something problematic like shackles or fatal like an axe. There was the Ansyran though. Subtly, he eased his gaze the man's way. A kick or punch from him could finalize anyone's last will and testament.

Desmond's throat jerked in an involuntary swallow.

"Yes, yes." Two sharp monosyllables from the prince clashed into Laudilas' droning words. It took another "yes" to silence the man completely. The prince didn't grace him with an "excuse me." Instead, with a dismissive wave of his hand that ended in a curling of thin fingers against his palm, he did what no plan or footstep had done all evening—he brought them to the crux.

"I know your surname." He was looking at Laudilas. "I'm aware of how many of our ancestors wedded and bedded, even stabbed each other. You don't need to tell me. And you—" Dark eyes darted to lock on Desmond's. "I know exactly how many gold hydras you have in the bank on Via dell'Oro. What I don't know is how well you can entertain me."

Silence followed almost as quickly as the words had come.

"Excuse me, Your Highness?" Desmond was surprised to hear the voice was his own. Laudilas was silent. Apparently, actors didn't know what to do when the audience decided to write their own script.

"You're loreborn. You plant, you war, you live, you die, just like anyone else. But no one can entertain quite like you." The prince's lips pulled into a small smile. Maybe it was meant to show he thought himself clever, but the smile was just a sad thing really, if a mother were to take it in.

But Desmond was no mother. *And you're not* seeing *either.*

Another silence.

With a grunt mixed with a hiss, Luca shifted, pushing himself up a little straighter. Roses rustled on either side of him. His smile had drained and apparently taken his patience with it. He tapped the diary's cover against that of the book in his lap. The sound had the same effect as a *tsk.* "Whichever one of you can succeed best in making me forget life for however briefly gets your national treasure. Fair?"

And there it is.

The words might have ended with a question mark, but the intention was clear. This was a verdict, nonnegotiable and final.

Laudilas didn't waste a second. "Your Highness is as cunning as he is gracious. A duel of stories. Yes, yes, this will go down in the annals of both our peoples. Shall I go first, Captain?"

The look Laudilas cast over his shoulder was like the shifting of pieces on a battle map. The young de Glas was the scion of kings and Desmond was the representative of all that royalty was not. Whatever had made him cling to Desmond like a child looking for home in a windstorm had vanished, and whatever had caused Desmond to respond to that need faded with one flare of royal brow.

Desmond waved him on. *Oh, don't mind me, I'll just be standing here panicking—trying to figure out how to juggle gold coins.*

Laudilas took two steps sideways, positioning himself so both the prince and the servants ringing the outer rim of the kitchen were spectators.

Hm, a backup audience. Clever.

The light from both the kitchen and the courtyard torches haloed him now, golden and bright. Then, with no fanfare or warning, Laudilas snapped his fingers. Each one, on both hands, cascaded in order against his thumbs.

Shadows sprang to life.

"Tonight," he began, "I will tell you the story of what you celebrate. Of your Mother, the Red Lady, Death herself. In the beginning—"

With deft quickness, the shadows were spun into forms. Dancers, ethereal and lithe. Time, Wisdom, Prudence, and two more. Their forms wove through the air as Laudilas began to tap his foot, pacing his shadow figures to a silent song.

"But then evil came into Creation, and Death was born." Another figure materialized from the darkness, but somehow, even as her figure joined the dance, darkness clung to her like a mantle made of soot and ashen weeds. Laudilas' foot slowed, its beat still steady but each tap had a foreboding edge now like a heartbeat that didn't know what might come next.

"The Creating God grieved for the ruin of his world and tried to overthrow the evil and the Darkness that had spawned it, but he could not cast him down. Overwhelmed and undone, he became only yet another victim of the fatal tempo Death had brought into a once glorious dance.

"Now there was nothing, no one standing between man and Darkness. But Death, she wept. The One Below had promised man so much, but the price for that pleasure, for that plenty, man could not pay. So, Death made a bargain—"

Desmond couldn't remember exactly what adherents of the Mother were called. The religion was so ingrained in every inch of Vawde culture, it simply just was.

Depressing *would be a good name for it.* Lies another. He knew Death. She took; she left nothing and she gave nothing.

And he had become just like her. He had nothing to give this prince. Even without *seeing*, he knew what sort of person sat before him: a young man broken by sickness, forgotten, alone, because he *too* had nothing to give—

Desmond turned from Laudilas and his shadow show so quickly, his neck whined in protest. Before he knew what he was doing, his eyes locked on the prince. Luca sat as he had before. Still, almost lifeless except for the rise and fall of his slender chest and the ocean raging in his eyes. Unable—or maybe unwilling—to stop himself, Desmond fell into it.

Fear, despair, anger hit him in cold, tangled waves. Fear of the future, despair of the present, and anger, so much anger over a past that Death's cold fingers had carved out in toying jabs from his young life.

Desmond pulled away, his heart pounding in his chest, his breath coming out in quick gasps as if he had actually been submerged in the sea. They were the same, he and this royal boy. Impossibly different and yet Death had robbed them the same. Luca hated this story. Desmond could see it in a sudden, hard twitch of his jaw.

"And so, Death became a mediator, a guardian of men. For those who please her, she intercedes—"

No. Desmond's feet started to move. He shouldn't be here. He shouldn't have come. He didn't wield words; he wielded weapons: swords, daggers...gold. None were what the prince wanted. None were what he needed.

There was nothing...nothing. His rushed footsteps pushed him through the outer kitchen, Laudilas' voice echoing unbroken behind him. The next kitchen was less crowded. Most of the inhabitants had gone out to see the two loreborn men perform. Maybe illusion would be enough to sate them.

He stopped. A lone person sat eating at a low table. And that's when he saw it. The Sagar violin from earlier, now resting as quiet and still as a babe in its crib. He swallowed involuntarily. His last violin had been shattered like a jilted maid's heart.

The musician who'd been playing the instrument sat hunched over a meal of fish and what looked like pasta drowned to a limp death in cream sauce.

A Sagar. That's what he'd said once around a campfire when he and three other knights had debated how they'd spend loot money. It was a dream he'd forgotten, snatched up and washed away by too much darkness.

But stolen things could be reclaimed. That's why they were here, wasn't it?

His hand moved before his mind could catch up or stop him. "It's yours, all of it." The note that had been inside Desmond's pocket was down on the table in less than a heartbeat. "I want to borrow that." He pointed to the violin.

The musician looked up at him, down at the paper with its tightly scrawled note, then just shrugged and went back to twirling his stringy meal. Desmond didn't wait for any further permission. He snatched up the case with something between haste and the utmost care.

Passing back into the open-faced kitchen, he set it down again. With a single hand, he grasped the buckle of his sword belt and unwove the latch in one quick motion. He did the same with the buttons that clasped the leather at his wrists. Shrugging off his jacket with its high, stiff collar, he chucked it along with his sword onto the sugar-coated table. For a moment, he stood there letting the night breeze tussle his shirtsleeves. If it had been a cold night, his breath would have frosted the air fast and heavy.

No blood. No bodies. That was the promise. That was the dream. Or was it?

As Laudilas' shadows danced across the red brick in the crescendo of their story, an honest truth rippled like a second wind through Desmond's soul. He wasn't a poor musician but his playing was no illusionist's show. A gambler wouldn't bet on his chances. But even if he couldn't reclaim the diary, maybe he could reclaim something else—

His dream had always been anything but death. Still, life could be wrenched from the jaws of this Dark Dancer in other ways...

Choose your weapon.

He unlocked the violin case and pulled the instrument out. The feel and weight of it in his hands was like holding a sword custom-made. The wood positively hummed with the echo of the tune it had sung earlier and with the yearning for another.

But what to play?

How did one put bow to strings and bring out life?

The fountain caught his eye as it spat and sprayed water into hungry air. Water, his old nemesis, the one thing that followed him everywhere: dirty, ever-flowing, never—

Dying.

The great scholars of the Veil said that water never died. It fell from the sky to the earth, only to rise up from the ground and seas and find its home in the clouds once again. An endless cycle.

He picked up the bow, still primed for playing.

"Thank you. A marvelous audience. Thank you."

Laudilas had finished now and was bowing as his shadows melted back into the night, leaving him alone in the spotlight of glory. Murmurs and applause surrounded the young man like roses tossed onto a stage. Only Luca didn't join. The prince merely nodded. Whether Laudilas took this as approval or encouragement to step aside, Desmond couldn't tell.

It was his turn now.

Either he was right or finally cracked up. With any luck, it would be both. The last one, at least, would get him a pass home.

He stepped forward, not quite taking Laudilas' place. He tucked the instrument between his shoulder and chin. His audience was the prince alone. Every musician played by their own rules. Some studied their audience, watching their reaction and playing to emotions. Some stared at a set of fixed spots and others closed their eyes, seeing nothing but the music. But Desmond saw only water.

With his index finger, he began to pluck at the strings. One note and then another and another. Each tone struck the air like water flowing rock by rock across a stony streambed. The sound was soft, the whispering rush of the wind mixed with it in tones almost like a harmony. Then he touched the bow to the strings and began to play.

The melody that came out was not one he'd played before. But he had heard it. In that backwater Chanti village with its muddy stream. Soft, faithfully trickling, undisturbed by the chaos of the world. As the water began to flow faster, his bow picked up pace with the dance of his fingers. It was a river now. The Alamein River back home that broadened mile by mile until it was a ribbon of blue silver, gurgling and rushing through the counties, twisting under bridges, passing through fields, and darting around castle towns. They had played there as children: Isa, Artair, and himself.

His eyes slid from the sound of his own memories to look at Luca. The boy probably had no idea what it was like to play ankle deep in mud chasing catfish. His fingers moved faster, his other arm sending more energy into his bow.

Measure by measure, the river went on.

Like a rogue, it spilled past the borders of Albidon, west into Atherland. Some said it was an arrow, piercing straight into their enemy's land as a constant reminder that what was loreborn could never be bound. Others said the cold river was chasing the warm embrace of the golden sunset.

Desmond had never seen where or how the river ended but there were stories.

Sliding his fingers closer to the bridge of the violin, the notes sang out higher, the bow rising and falling fast as it echoed the suspense. The rush of rapids running, running through hills and heathered moors, wild and free—

Until there was nothing, only water plunging down, tumbling over rock, water and air tangling in threaded notes of mist and thunder. Foot after foot, the Alamein fell. His wrist and fingers drove the notes out in vibrato as the water slid into a deep, still pool below.

The bow came up from the strings. He blinked. Around him, the world slowly came back into focus. Luca was moving, stumbling legs half pushed, half dragged from their resting place until he was sitting on the edge of the wall, one hand still locked around a knee while the other had caught hold of the lattice beside him. His eyes were fixed on Desmond.

Desmond swallowed, trying to remember the ending. A lake spilled out beyond the waterfall, ringed by evergreen pines. He let out a tight breath through his nose and started to pluck again. A middle note, a high one, then the middle again. Finally, without flourish and only a split heartbeat of pause, he struck a low note. It shivered in the air, like delicate waves lapping at a pebbled shore. It grew softer and softer until at last, it melted into the wind.

The applause that followed was more subdued than Laudilas had received, but it was better than silence. That was the hypothetical equivalent of rotten garbage flying your way for a performer. But Desmond barely noticed. Luca was still sitting on the edge of the wall. His thick eyebrows puckered like a calligrapher's *v*. Something wet trickled down the young man's cheek. He must really be in a weakened state if moving that little had made him sweat. Or was it...tears?

Before Desmond could decide and just as the last echoes of the applause faded, another took its place. Loud, solitary and worse than rotten garbage. Desmond's heel ground against the brick as he turned to face the newcomer.

"Little brother, there you are."

Little was the right word, but not for Luca. Haloed in the same light Laudilas had used earlier, though with none of the effect, stood a small, sandy-haired man, of indeterminate age but very determinate weight.

"You've kept all the best entertainment for yourself. Then again, you always did know how to make yourself everyone's favorite. Everyone but your mother, that is." This last sentence, the newly arrived royal spoke almost under his breath, but everyone heard it all the same. Whatever Luca's reaction to Desmond's performance had been was washed away by a look of venom so pure, it could have slain a dragon with one drop.

"Enzo." The name ground out from the younger prince's mouth more like a warning than a greeting.

The short man ignored the tone. "These are loreborn. You can't *pick* a winner. It must be a vote! Long live the storytellers' republic!" He gave a mock salute with a hand so heavily jeweled it was nigh impossible to believe he had the muscles to hold it up. "Poor boy." Enzo cast a glance from Laudilas to Desmond. "The mind, you know." A ringed finger tapped against his temple. "Can't be expected to be sharp when the body isn't."

An older sibling antagonizing the crippled one. How Drake. How cliché. Desmond might have lauded himself on the utter predictability of the scene before him if he wasn't so busy wondering if the finger could suddenly turn into a woodpecker's beak and drill a hole into the man's skull. If something magical didn't shut this newcomer up, he was going to see to it that something practical did.

But Luca just gave a wave of his own hand. It looked like a surrender flag, pale skin set against the midnight sky, but something devious gleamed in the young man's eyes. "By all means," he said. "Enlighten us as to how it's done." His lips had curled into a smile but there was nothing genuine about it.

"Well." The word came out with the bluster that was quickly fading from Enzo's ruddy face. "Well!" He turned to the servants. "You. Which one did you like the most? The shadow show I caught the last seconds of or this musician. He played well enough. Eh? Show of hands, now! Come, don't be shy. You, cupbearer boy, what do you think?"

Desmond turned away. Even with the poor sell the prince had given Laudilas, he knew who the crowd would choose.

Sliding the violin back into its case, he began to reassemble his own wardrobe. He was buckling on his sword when the verdict came in.

Laudilas bowed enough times to give an empty skull a concussion. To the dispersing servants. To Enzo.

Luca handed him the diary without a word. Instead, he directed his gaze to his brother. "Brilliant," he said, words dripping and laced. "People just adore being forced to give opinions. That's exactly how it works in Albidon, I'm sure. Right, de Glas?" He finally looked at Laudilas, putting particular emphasis on the surname. Laudilas just bowed again, mumbling something that sounded a good deal like nothing.

Desmond chuckled to himself as he set to snapping the locks on the violin's case. He'd have to find that musician again. For a brief moment, a feeling of regret gnawed at him. *Borrow? Should have said purchase*. Either way, the stupid gold was off his hands.

He gave one last look over his shoulder. Laudilas had left, a vanishing streak of silver and blue. The Merced, however, had stepped back into sight. He was leaning over Luca. Whatever he was saying had pulled all emotion from the prince's face like the locking of a vaulted safe. If thoughts of pillows and clean sheets weren't filling his vision more and more with each blink, Desmond might have been curious. There was something strange about this night. Dulled as they were, his senses were still rippling with the feeling of something he couldn't quite put his finger on.

Bah, royals and their games.

Picking up the case, he dropped a bow in Luca's direction. The young man wouldn't see it but maybe Laudilas had rubbed off on him a little—or maybe, maybe he cared. He was too tired to feel and understand the emotions this night and his actions had brought. Doubtless they would demand attention later.

To his surprise, when he straightened, his eyes met with the prince's. Luca smiled. Unlike his barbs or clever manipulations, there was something unique about the expression. Like a jewel rarely seen and even more rarely given.

And maybe that was reward enough. Not for Albidon perhaps. Not for Artair. But in that moment, Desmond didn't care.

One thing he had to acknowledge, and it wasn't a feeling, but rather the lack of one. To see was to hurt, but it was also to be what he cherished most. Alive. Free. Blindness was a prison; a cold heart was a grave.

As he turned to go, his own lips tugged into something resembling a smile of their own. And for the first time in a long time, its light reached even his eyes.

PhantomRien.

PhantomRin.

NINE

KENNET

The lone gondola bobbing in the water, the Mother's statue cold in its repose, the figure inside the gondola—

Nightingale.

The word fluttered against the bars of unconsciousness that trapped his mind. It went with an image engraved on the back of a book the figure had held, the last thing he remembered seeing before the drug had taken him. The figure had a name—

"Wake up, Immortal. Naptime's over." A rough hand patted his cheek.

"Oh, for mercy's sake, be polite about it."

That last voice, a little farther away than the first—it belonged to the name. Kennet's eyes flew open as he surged upright, smacking away the hand and taking Luca's Ansyran bodyguard tumbling with him over the edge of a narrow bed. His bed.

Wait.

He blinked, taking in his surroundings. This was his home. Vawde, superstitious as they were, didn't go down into the ruins of their old city. And they definitely never went even further underground into the primeval Under, a world built deep beneath the earth with craftsmanship few now remembered.

He had been amazed how much of the Under had survived the destruction of the original empire—even if half that destruction was now crammed into its vaulted halls and alcoves—but he had made it home. It was like him: ancient and forgotten—

Except, someone apparently had remembered too much.

With the Ansyran still pinned beneath him, he looked up at Luca. There was no book in his hands now. "What have you done?" The snarl thundered out of him like blazing fodder from a cannon's mouth. His limbs still felt numb and his mind foggy, but he knew enough.

I'm not the one standing in your way.

No. Death hadn't been.

Luca was.

But why?

The prince didn't meet his gaze or answer his words. Not right away. He sat in a small outcropping cut into the shortest of the alcove's rocky walls. It was shaped so a man might have commanded it like a throne if they'd been so disposed. But Luca had curled himself in the nook like a cat, and like a cat, he was looking outside.

This particular alcove was made of three dove-grey rock walls, but the fourth wall was nothing but the briny depths of the sea. Almost. A wide, thick panel of meridian glass, almost nine feet tall and equally as wide was all that stood between the chamber and living blue water beyond. An otherworldly and spectacular sight, a hidden world right before one's very eyes.

Schools of fish streamed like dancers through the water, and just outside the glass, half embedded, half swirling, was the deteriorating wreckage of at least one ship, maybe more. A handful of coins spun up from the sandy bottom and were swept away in an eddy of water and puffer fish.

"What have you done?" Kennet found himself repeating the question, this time in a gasp, casting it out like a tattered net trying to catch something before it floated too far out of reach. His plan. Desperately, he looked to the window. He could see daylight, faint but golden, trickling down through the water. It had been afternoon, the beginning of a storm, when he'd passed out. This window faced east meaning it had to be near sunrise now.

The entire evening. The entire *night*—gone.

This time, Luca answered.

"What you weren't doing," he said. The words were soft, cracked with a strange weariness.

But Kennet barely registered any of it. With wooden movements, he stood, pulling the Ansyran up with him. The man gave no protest, despite having easily taken him earlier. As soon as Kennet's hand released from his collar, the big man darted into the shadows. Whatever was about to happen, he seemed to want no part of it.

"And *what* exactly wasn't I doing?" But Kennet didn't wait for an answer. He didn't want one. Grinding his heel against the smooth floor, he moved towards the fireplace. The absence of swish around his heels told him someone had divested him of his long coat. Tea. He wanted tea.

A weak fire coughed in the hearth. He threw a glance over his shoulder that could have passed for an eye roll. Whichever one of these Fall-ruined idiots had tried to coax the flames to life apparently had no idea how a fireplace deep underground channeled out its smoke. He jabbed at the logs with a poker while his other hand reached up to shift a loose stone sticking out from the mantel.

The fire roared to life like a drowning man that had found air. He felt his emotions flame with it. *Fall and ruin.* He *did* want answers and they were going to be crisped to ashes, whatever they were.

Luca was the brother, blood and soul twin, to the Mediatrix, the current face of all Kennet sought to destroy. When he'd first taken a position on the prince's staff, he had expected to find himself in the center of Red Seat activity, a quick and easy way to scope out his opposition.

But over the weeks, Luca had shown little to no interest in his sister's minions. *Bah.* The boy's religious apathy had made him too comfortable. Blinded him to the obvious. Even if Luca had no reverence for Death, he would protect his sister. To Vawde, duty to family was everything.

He gave the logs one final stab before turning back around, the desire for tea forgotten. Luca had shifted in the nook. He sat now like the royal he was and there was no flinch in his slender frame as Kennet approached.

"I'm not your enemy, Immortal," the prince finally said when only four paces remained between them, his voice still startlingly ragged, contrasting with his posture. "But"—an edge of threat crept in—"I suggest you start showing me you're not mine."

Kennet's arms slid across his chest, fingers beginning to knead at his biceps. "And what *exactly* would make me your enemy?"

Luca's lips twitched, knowingly. "You'd like to see the Red Seat take center stage in hell."

Smart boy. "I'm not against pushing it along to its destination, no." Kennet moved a pace closer but to the side. Just because he couldn't die didn't mean he enjoyed people's attempts to make him try. "But." Another question cut into line before the others in his mind. "You're calling me 'Immortal.' What makes you think so?"

Luca's smile turned into the faintest chuckle. "You didn't die the other night, did you?"

The other night? The knife attack just before he'd met with the spymistress... *"What?"* Kennet whirled to see the Ansyran in the shadows spinning a very singular and very recognizable dagger delicately between his fingers.

Fall and ruin.

His breath tangled in his throat. "You could have killed me! What if you'd been wrong?"

Luca's gaze leveled at him like a crossbow with its target sighted. "I'm never wrong." Then he shrugged. "But I'm also not always right. I had to be sure."

Kennet choked out an explosive huff. This was insanity. Pure madness. But after a thousand years, he should have known better. The Vawde mind saw the world as a chessboard. People were pieces and ambition was channeled in moves.

Games. That's what life was in the Masque. Maybe this boy didn't even care about his sister. Maybe this was just sport to him, something to sate his Drake blood and make him feel that, in at least one thing, he had gained the upper hand. That even a cripple could reach out far enough to sink his claws into someone. And Kennet had been that *very* lucky person.

But there were men's games and there were children's games, and this was about as juvenile as they came. The future of a race's spiritual freedom was at stake, and here he was, cut off by a bored boy.

His temper snapped like dried twigs in an inferno. He stepped forward until only a mere pace separated him from the object of his fury. If frustration of the highest degree would have a mental shade for him in the centuries to come, it would probably be the memory of this moment.

"Do you think I pass my immortality by making daisy chains and dancing a jig with every fiddler who happens by? No. Oh, no. I may have time but others around me do not, and I have a purpose—"

"Will you listen to me!"

Kennet blinked. Luca had surged upright, putting his face mere inches away. Standing, he was even taller than one might have guessed. The prince's white-knuckled grip strangled the rock beneath his thin fingers. It was hard to tell if it was his legs or sheer force of will keeping him upright.

"Please." His voice cracked again but this time the sound sliced the air like thunder in the storm. Tears chased down his cheeks in a downpour. "For the love of God, just listen to me."

The words about to come out of Kennet's mouth scrambled back down his throat. But not even a flood of tears could douse the flames of his anger completely. "What?" he barbed instead. "God? You're Vawde. God is supposed to be dead to you."

Luca's chest expanded with a shuddering heave, the gold embroidered into his doublet twinkling with the movement. He dashed the wet from his face. "You're proving my point with your own mouth." Narrowing his eyes until there was no past or future in his gaze, only that very moment, he went on. "Look at me. If you won't listen, *look*.

"I don't think I've taken a breath my entire life without pain somewhere in my body, but I wasn't always like this—" He gave a brief but disgusted glance down at his wasted legs that trembled with the effort of him holding him up. "Once I could go where I wanted to. I had plans and dreams. But when the time came for me to change from boy to man, I became something else instead. This faith my people have? I don't need faith to know Death is real. Her voice whispers in my ear, sometimes loud, sometimes far off, but always, she's there. Someone like me is easy prey. And I hate her for it.

"But—but I hate the dark even more." The confession came out in a whisper, not like he was afraid to say it, but as if the mere thought brought more pain than even someone like him wanted to acknowledge. Shifting backwards slightly, but still standing, he let the rock face take more of his weight and went on.

"I used to love the stars," he said, eyes flickering away from Kennet to focus on a spot in the shadows. "I thought as a boy someday I'd go to Yeurik'yin and study the heavens. But then, the dark came to me instead and the stars didn't come with it.

"I was so sick, even something as dim as candlelight was a torment." A pucker flickered across his brow at the memory. "Light made my head ring like the clapper in a tower bell. Trying to focus on words or even faces sent my stomach spinning. So, I was left in the dark, cut off from everything I'd once loved. For two years, I was like that. It's—it's cold in the dark, you know." Long-fingered hands reached up to rub absently at his arms.

"Behind Death is the Darkness. We're taught this from the earliest age. Sometimes, when I'd lie there with nothing to see but the insides of my own eyelids, it felt like there was another layer to the colorless void, something—someone just waiting to swallow me whole. Like an abyss you could fall into and never rise again. Death is real. Darkness is real.

"But I knew," he said, hands sliding away from his arms to wrap tightly around his waist, "I knew that even if I couldn't see them anymore, the stars were still in the sky each night. I knew even if all I felt was the stale air of the same room day after day, somewhere the sun was still warm."

His eyes finally found Kennet's again, voice strengthening with the conviction of his words. "Clouds aren't blots erasing the stars no matter how dark the night is, and even a hurricane can't rage hard enough to rip the sun from the sky. So, I knew what I'd been told to believe since I was a boy, I knew it couldn't be true. Darkness can't defeat Light."

A weary, almost bitter laugh escaped his lips. "I doubt I'm very good at it, believing in a God, a living, redeeming one. But if you've been in my company for four months and haven't noticed I try— How loud do I have to scream?" He finally collapsed back onto the seat. "You're proving my point," he repeated.

Kennet felt his vision spin. "What point?" The words were kicked out of his mouth by the sudden burst of breath he had been holding. The room spun again. Maybe it was the aftereffects of the drug, or—

"Maybe you came back from death, however the legend goes, to tell people's stories," Luca answered. "But you aren't very good at actually caring about people. At least not here.

"Ideas are soulless and bloodless, nobody dies in an argument. But *from* an argument?" He glanced at the blue water. "I'm surprised every time I see the ocean. I wonder why it's not red. When you take all that the Red Seat proclaims to hell, will you take those who believe it blindly —or even with both eyes open—will you take them, too? Will you destroy them just for what they believe? Don't their souls deserve a chance?"

Kennet looked at the boy before him like a man who has stared at a painting all day thinking he finally comprehended every line of it only to realize he'd been looking at the piece upside down the entire time. He blinked.

"It's probably not my place to judge or do what I did," Luca went on in a sighing tone that said he was pacing with his voice since his legs could not. "But I know what it's like to become a thing instead of a human. To be seen as the embodiment of a list of problems and not a living soul. When you can't answer, even to blink back or squeeze a hand, people stop talking to you. Oh, they talk about you, around you, over you. But—"

He leaned forward, elbows bent and slender hands draped white-knuckled over his knees. "You're still in there, locked away, a part of you screaming to be heard somehow, to be seen again.

"I'm begging you—I got in your way, made my own plan because—because red, heart-beating blood is not the same color as coal-black lies. They're different. Separate. Do you see that?" His eyes bored into Kennet's.

Kennet felt his legs buckle. Sagging into a small outcropping that jutted out to Luca's left, he sat with a heavy thump. "You think I'm out to harm your sister," he said quietly. This alone felt certain in his mind. This was a young man defending a sister, not out of some innate sense of duty. But because...he cared?

Saints and sinners, a Vawde with a heart? Something rarer than rubies or even miracles.

Luca only shrugged. "I haven't really seen Magdalena since we were five and her power manifested. If it's her choice to go down in the flames, that's on her. But I want her to at least go knowing there was a way out. She was human once. Still is. I don't suppose you even knew she had a name." He arched an eyebrow knowingly. "That's what the Red Seat does to even their own leader, scrubs away everything you are until all that's left is a smiling face with the unfathomable power to manipulate minds. You're corroding others' freewill and don't even know what's happened to your own.

"But it's not just about her. What about the old flower seller by the east dock or the newest child born to a noble house? You were here before me and you will still live long after any of us are gone. But, we—we were real. We *are* real."

At this, silence fell across the alcove. Luca sat still leaning forward, but his shoulders had taken on a hunched look. Kennet blinked again, Luca's words swirling through his mind like a whirlwind unsure where—if—it would land.

"Do you know the story of the red dragon and the white? The ones painted over your doorway?" he finally asked. It was the barest of movements, but he could have sworn the prince's shoulders tensed.

"When I was young, a long time ago, my wife—well, she wasn't my wife then, she was just a loreborn storyteller I'd met on the street. Anyway, she used to tell this tale of a great battle that was coming someday. But it wouldn't be led by men. Instead, two dragons will fight in the sky. One red as blood and the other pale as the moon. Whether their war would last long or short, she couldn't say.

"From the red dragon's mouth will come shadow, not fire. And the white dragon will have no flame at all. Shadow after shadow will blast from the red dragon, cloaking the sun and dimming the light from this world.

"But then the white dragon will come. And, hour by hour, he will stand blowing the shadows away with every simple breath of his body and pulse of his powerful wings. No one knows if this battle will last until the end of days—or if one day, the white beast will finally blow away both shadow and dragon, changing the world and taking things from the past into the future.

"People always believed this was an Athlander story. They're the home of the dragons, after all. But when your family became the first Vawde house to declare that they would be the ones to take that unconquerable kingdom, when you took the name Drake for yourselves, the story went with you. Just another stolen thing a Vawde family was trying to claim was meant for them. They were the white dragons, the ones who would bring a bloodless conquest. A ridiculous promise." Kennet snorted. "But maybe—"

His gaze swept over the young man before him. A weak boy, with no glory of his own, born opposite of another who strode through this world leeching light from the souls of men with the darkest of shadow. *Maybe this is who I'm looking for?*

But Luca interrupted his thought. "Stop," he said softly, but his tone was heavy like the dropping of a hammer. "Stop trying to plan the future. Maybe Albidon will come save us one day. That was your scheme, right? The nightingale on the back of the loreborn queen's diary, it's their symbol of freedom." He smiled faintly, like something in recent memory amused him. "Yes, they do like doing things their own way.

"But—" He finally leaned back, a grimace sweeping across his face as he did so. He shook his head. "An army can't save a city that doesn't even know it needs a rescue. They could, I suppose, but that's just another conquest, not liberation. Isn't that the point? Freedom? Freewill?

"But simple people can save people, if they see a need, make the choice. But it won't be an orderly game. Wildcards, Immortal, you can't predict them, you can't prophesy them. Just because you're more certain of making it into the future than any of the rest of us doesn't mean you can control what happens even in something as close as tomorrow."

"They killed me." The cutting words came out in a flash. Kennet could hardly believe them as they left his mouth. A sudden, hot fire exploded in his chest, driving him to his feet. Not like the one before. No, this was a wildfire spreading through his veins, clashing with the whirlwind that was every reasoning, every truth Luca had said.

Revenge. That's what Death had said. That's what the voice had answered those hours ago. And yes, maybe, stripped bare and honest, that *was* what he wanted. Ruin for ruin.

But the prince didn't flinch before the flames. "And in the past few hours, they killed dozens more," he said. "I wager if you look out into the water, you'll see their ashes sinking down." His hand flung out, the long, slashed sleeve of his doublet spilling open to reveal intricate golden stitching. His knuckles struck the glass with a hard *thwack.*

But Luca's words were only kindling to the fire. "I don't want—" Kennet ground his nails deep into his palm. "Someday, I don't want to be the only one left. If this doesn't stop, it will keep spreading, kingdom by kingdom, generation by generation. Darkness is strong. I can't live in a world without hope and goodness."

"Then don't be the only one left. Tell me, Immortal, why did they kill you?"

"For believing what I wanted, and not what I was told," came Kennet's swift reply. It was a fancy answer. One he'd written once in the opening of a diary he'd long since lost. But still, the words were the truth.

"Yes." Luca nodded, the dry, faint smile from earlier back on his face. "But I'm pretty sure what you were thinking on the inside wasn't as provoking as something else? What was it? What happens," he pressed, "to a child born in a storm? With no sun, no stars. Someone has to tell them that they're real. Whisper in their ear that sunsets really come, that the north star really will take you home. You have to tell people what's true when they can't see it.

"Revenge is like stabbing someone in the chest who once stabbed you in the back. It's pain for pain. But there's something sharper in this world and that's fear. What sets the Red Seat's knees knocking is the truth. So—" The word shot out like an arrow, swift and true. "Open your mouth and make them afraid.

"What?" he chuckled after a moment's pause. "Just because I'm weak, do not presume I am kind. I've lost people I love to the Red Seat too." Luca's tone took a sudden, harsh shift. "And maybe I'll live to see them get justice or maybe I'll be turned to ashes just like them.

"I want this to end, just like you, no matter what it takes. The lies, though. Not the people. But they have to know that Death isn't the only answer. That there is this hope you love, this redemption they think was lost. This God they believe failed. They have to know the *real* story."

With that Luca fell silent, his expression fading to blankness. His hands curled themselves together against his palms in loose fists. "And that's all I have to say," he finally said in the same quiet, ragged tone he'd used in the beginning.

Kennet took a step forward, arms sliding into a cross against his chest. The fire surging through him was snuffing itself out flame by flame. There was rain inside that whirlwind of words and fire could not stand against rain. Just like darkness was always swallowed by light... but only if someone was brave enough to keep striking the match again and again...

"Who decided you could be so wise?" he asked softly. He blinked, but not in another attempt to figure this young royal out, not this time. There were tears staining his vision.

Luca rolled his eyes. "I've had an insufferable amount of time to think. And I mean that in all the ways you can break down that adjective."

Kennet Zur was used to two things: being one of the tallest people in the room, and most certainly being the oldest. He swallowed, a small part of him mentally cursing that he'd stopped in the middle of making tea. He was not used to being wrong. And even less accustomed to anyone telling him he was.

"I didn't know you thought my stories were so amazing," he finally said.

Luca shrugged. "Never said I did. There's nothing fancy about them. You're no illusionist."

Kennet's lips flattened. His wife had been able to weave stories with blooms and vines. A sudden wave of longing rose inside him. Oh, to see that wild grace of storytelling...that smile one more time. He forced his throat to scrape down another dry swallow, taking the ancient memories with it. One of the two sent to retrieve the old queen's diary must have been an illusionist. He wondered what their affinity was.

"But a story doesn't need flash and show to reach the heart," Luca was saying. "Truth has its own power whether it's boomed from a palace rooftop or whispered in a hovel. Just tell your stories, Immortal. The ones you know, the ones happening—" With a sudden gasp, the prince doubled forward, palm pressing hard against his left hip.

Kennet flung out a hand to catch him just as a form effervesced beside him. The Ansyran. Chords, he'd forgotten the man was even here. "What's wrong with him?" Kennet asked. He had never seen Luca show such pain so openly. But then, he'd also never seen the young man outside the safety of his own chambers.

"Couldn't say," the man grunted. "You've seen his sideboard. Probably some witch's brew he's been too long without. Here, let me take him."

The Ansyran reached out, but Kennet shifted, blocking him. Lifting the prince into his own arms with one swift movement, he jerked his head away from the window and even further east. "I know a way into the palace that's quicker than any route you used." Then without waiting to see if he was followed, he swept from the room.

Luca was a strange burden. Half limp limbs and wasted muscles mixed with the stiffness of a brace that clamped his back and chest into a rigid line. "Who are you trying to impress with such posture, boy," Kennet muttered to the semi-conscious form slumped against his shoulder. Luca's only answer was a faint snort that trailed off into a moan.

Kennet lengthened his strides. "Did you know," he went on, footfalls clicking softly on the smooth stone beneath his feet, "that the sun is a star too? Stay with me just a little longer, just up these stairs, and I'll show you the sunrise like you've never seen it before."

It was a sight he had passed by scores of times, maybe hundreds. But today, Kennet paused as the stone stairwell led them into a long passageway. The entire corridor, panel after panel, was made of occulus glass, from the arched ceiling, even the floor.

Unlike meridian glass, occulus had been forged from the sands of the Saar Isles that lay far beyond the Ring of Ice in the north. It reflected and refracted both the light above and the water surrounding it, splitting and mixing them both into exotic rainbows of colors that trailed through the air like a thousand ethereal ribbons.

Kennet heard Luca let out a gasp. His head didn't move, but the look in the prince's eyes told that the sound came, not from pain, but from wonder. A ray of pure golden hue mixed with a strand of cloud white fluttered before them. Luca's fingers loosened from their grip on Kennet's tunic to reach out and let the light dance through the weave of his hand.

Kennet couldn't help but notice the strand of white despite the brilliance that surrounded him. That old Athlander tale—the white dragon— Maybe he hadn't been wrong. Maybe the tension that had been in Luca's shoulders when he'd told the story said, deep down, he knew it too.

As he carried the prince on further up into the blooming morning light, the thought continued to rumble through his mind. Maybe it was rebellious to think on it, a last flame still unwilling to surrender just yet. Or maybe it was the truth.

Because, after all, dragons weren't made to walk. They were made for something else—

They were made to fly.

TEN

Laudilas

Laudilas would have skipped—if he wasn't past twenty and so bone weary.

The sun was rising now, its warm face crowning the horizon like a golden coin chipped in half.

No one was happy to see it.

La Notte della Dama Rosa ended with the dawn. Death's time of grace was over. Laude stood at the end of a bridge, watching citizen after citizen hand over a penny and take a red paper mask from a cart. Masks were always a popular fashion here; the plain or elaborate face coverings had given the city its name centuries ago. But no one wore them on La Notte. There was no sin to hide and no great one's judgment to hide it from. But the morning after was a different story...

Guilt swam through the muggy air. Laude could taste it. It rolled in waves off the citizens around him and wormed through his senses, delving deep. He rubbed at his temple. He shouldn't feel this way. He'd won. He moved his hand to knock a fist against his heart. The diary was still there, tucked between his silk tunic and his surcoat. He knocked again. The hollow sound that thumped in answer felt more genuine than a true heartbeat.

Dancing, downing liquors that hailed from as far east as Uroshii Under the Moon and as far west as the Neverknown, that was how he'd spent from midnight to dawn. There had even been kissing. At least he hoped that was the reason a faint red stain came away as his other hand rubbed at his lower lip. *Or is it blood?* A blurry memory of flying fists darted through his mind. He felt his lip again. It didn't matter. He was too numb to feel pain. Numb was natural. *Numb is good.* Now if he could only will his mind to feel the same.

He pushed through the crowd pressing around the cart. He didn't need a mask. He rolled his shoulders, letting his neck swivel in a twist to loosen the stiffness there. Bad idea. The bridge suddenly writhed before him like an angry snake.

He grabbed for the railing, forcing his eyes to focus on the cold, dark canal water below instead. Beside him, a child started to fuss. With a spiteful thrust, the little one let his new red mask drop into the water. Laude heard the mother curse. He wondered what sins the family had committed that they wanted to hide even a child's face.

When does it end? How many more sins, stabs in the back, tricks and twists? How much longer would this sometimes-silent, sometimes-loud war between his family and their people last? He watched as the dye bled from the discarded mask, turning a spot in the water red.

It was just a little spot. Last night had just been a small thing, just a book. Like Edenry had said, there had been no blood, no bodies. Not now. Not yet. But there would be.

Someone tapped his shoulder from behind. He turned, stomach cursing at the sudden movement. An old man, with a gap-toothed grin, stood behind him holding out a mask. Laude waved him off with a tight-lipped smile of his own and started down the other side of the bridge.

He knew who he was. What he was. Why hide it?

He was a dog.

Benerict was the master.

Every step through that palace had whispered the truth to him. Even the thrill of the shadows bending to his storytelling hadn't erased the nagging knowledge completely. And the rising dawn had ripped down the last of his mental defenses.

A dog. Sometimes, he was the little sibling who did tricks on the stage, his cute, fluffy aura a good contrast to his warrior brother. But other times, he was the retriever. The pageboy dog who chased what Benerict had lost or found too far out of reach.

A gust of wind caught his coat's train, whipping it out around his knees like a turret flag. Two young women just stepping onto the bridge darted out of his way. For once, he didn't spare them a second glance.

The dead body was still outside his room when he cleared the second-floor landing of the Rex and Rod. But it sat propped against the wall now, eyes closed, hands reverently folded in its lap.

Benerict.

Laude shoved the door open with a kick. But it wasn't Benerict who greeted him.

"Little Laudie de Glas!" a battle-roughened voice called out.

A stocky man sat astride the trunk that held Laude's possessions. His clothes were travel stained, the front of his tunic emblazoned with an unmistakable insignia. He flashed Laude a smile, but there was nothing inviting or charming about it. In fact, the silvery unsheathing of a sword probably had a more welcoming effect than that baring of teeth.

Laude groaned. Nathair Mallory, general of the Albidoni West Regulars. He was the lovable sort—if someone liked drought, plague, rotten meat, and bad stories. And here he was. In the flesh. In Laude's room. On his trunk.

"My lord Mallory," he said, stepping into the room and sweeping a bow, the movement as automatic as if he were a puppet on strings—or a dog on a leash. *Always please the Albidoni lords, never show emotion—*

A key flew at him. He caught sight of it just as a dull glint of brass began to sail past his ear. He flung out a hand to catch it, but the white plaster walls of the room spun as his head turned. His fingers grasped air; his knees wobbled, then kissed the floor with a dull smack followed by both hands.

Nathair ignored him. "Your brother said you've got a dagger you're looking to sell. I want to see it."

—always curb your tongue. No command on bootlicking could stop his mind from exploding, though. *Chords in flats and sharps in every key. Chords.* Laude swallowed back the pain shooting through his palms, forcing down the angry words that had bloomed with it. "I don't have it anymore," he finally managed to mutter.

Gingerly, he lifted his head. He needed something to pull himself up with. Nathair didn't move to help. The man just shrugged from where he sat, a look of strange disappointment on his craggy face. *There.* Barely within reach was the footboard of the bed, but Laudilas made a grab for it, heaving himself upright with a single slipped-out curse.

He remembered that dagger. It had belonged to one of his uncles, the royal insignia of House de Glas carved into the hilt. He'd lost it in a game of lore 'n' lies weeks ago. Ever since, he'd been terrified Benerict would find out. But...if his brother was volunteering its sale, maybe he didn't care about it as much as Laude had thought.

Truth be told, Laude had never been serious about selling it anyway. The threat had only been a little growl, a little showing of the teeth when Benerict had once yanked his chain too tight.

Now that he was standing again, he took a step towards his trunk. His eyebrows and mouth curved into a hinting arch. *Get your carcass off my belongings.* But the general just drummed his fingers across the trunk's scratched lid in response, eyes fixed somewhere just beside the window.

Laude let his breath snort out silently through his nose. He didn't know why he was surprised. Or why he'd bothered. This was Nathair's way. Stretching out a foot behind himself, Laude let the tapping toe of his boot start searching for his key.

When Albidon had overthrown their royal family those many years ago, the person to lead the way had been the king's own steward, Chaucer Seymere. After that, the man had become some sort of hero-leader to the people. They called him the Unmaker. But about a decade ago, Seymere had fallen ill. So, to show their deep gratitude for all he'd done, the Albidoni had dumped the man on his sick bed and ran off looking for another hero.

They set up a tourney, the Tourney of Faces as it came to be known. Whoever won would win the hearts of the people.

The eighteen-year-old Count of Prenzlau had claimed the victory that day. With a smile more brilliant than even the gold of his hair, Artair had accepted the peoples' cheering adoration.

But where there is a winner, there is a loser.

There. He snatched up the slender key and buried it in his fist.

Nathair had been that loser, and the general had taken his defeat at the hands of a beanpole-built boy about as well as a flood takes more water. Fights had broken out in taverns and whispers had swirled in the streets. But a few short weeks later, none of it had mattered anyway. Seymere surprised his fickle followers and took back both his health and his seat of power again.

But Artair was not so easily forgotten. Year by year, the peoples' eyes had shifted more and more towards his leadership. They called him their Godsent, the prophesied one who would bring the gilded age.

Nathair didn't send his thugs to rough up Artair's Falcons at their suppers anymore, but, like a dog marking his territory, the man now took whatever he could: land, lovers, gold. The taxes his fenland tenants were forced to pay was gossiped to be the highest in the country.

He was like Benerict. Both wanted what someone else said they could not have. He was also like a dog—

"Oh, there you are." Benerict's soft tenor sounded in the doorway, cutting off any compatriotic feelings Laude might have just started feeling towards his visitor. “Someone should do something about that body. It’s disrespectful to just leave him there.”

But not disrespectful that he was killed in the first place?

“We’re going home. Where’s the diary?”

Despite himself, Laude’s emotions flickered again. The confidence with which Benerict had said that last line, like it wasn’t truly a question. He really did believe Laude had gotten what he’d been sent for. But that first sentence—

“Home?” He threw a look first to his brother, then to the general who still sat straddling his trunk.

“Yes.” The elder de Glas stepped into the room and moved to stand by its single, narrow window. “Imperator’s orders. Our army is being sent home and Lord Mallory’s”—he gave a back jerk of his head in the general direction of the trunk—“is taking our place. And this room apparently.”

With that, Benerict turned to look at Nathair. He blinked as if just as confused as Laude had been about the man’s current resting place but understanding never flickered in his eyes. Benerict wasn’t that sort of man. “Why” wasn’t a word in his dictionary.

Nathair broke the awkward silence. “So, what’s he look like, this imperator? I met the one before him. Did you know that one was actually a younger brother to this one? But different mothers. Hmm, Alfonse had a sort of mainland Camrai complexion.” Nathair waved a hand at his own face. “What about this one?”

Benerict’s bewildered expression deepened. “His Imperial Majesty’s mother is from Atherland?” The reply came out as a question, the kind of answer one gives when they can't fathom why someone would ask the original question in the first place.

"Ah." Nathair shifted so his back scraped against the peeling plaster of the wall. "Pale face, then." He looked bored, unsated. With a grunt, he swung his booted feet onto the bed.

Laude winced as dried mud scattered across the cream quilt. So much for "always please the Albidoni lords." "What's wrong with that?" he found himself saying, a quick laugh coming out with the words, nervous and edgy. "Most royal families' bloodlines are about as mixed as a back-alley mongrel. An alchemical nightmare."

At this, Nathair chuckled, a deep sound that reverberated against his folded arms. "Better than bedding your snot-nosed sister, eh? Like the Saar? I like this one, de Glas." He jerked his chin in Laude's direction. "Beg and barter hard about making *him* king and we all might just follow along."

Better yet, tie me to a wheel and break every bone in my body. I'll thank you more. Laude didn't bother to look Benerict's way. He could feel the sudden, hot reaction from where he stood. Only one thing could break his brother's singular focus on the crown and that was the insinuation that *if* there was going to be a crown, it should be on someone else's head. Rarely did people suggest Laude was the better option, but each time, it was like having a thousand flaming arrows pointed at one target—himself.

He didn't like it.

"So." He moved to the other side of the room, yanking on the top latch of a tall but narrow chest of drawers. But even from here, he could feel Benerict's jealous gaze following him. "Are d'Argon and the Falcons staying?" *If you don't want to be the target, find a bigger one.*

Nathair let out a string of bone-rattling expletives. Between that and Benerict's own mental firestorm, maybe the room would just explode and save them all the bother. Laude closed his eyes and tuned out whatever was happening behind him.

Reaching into his surcoat, he pulled out the diary and looked at it. The front was of a simple design, latched closed with an old brass lock. He turned it over. The gilding was faded now but he could just make out the outline of a bird stretched in flight. A nightingale?

He tossed the book onto the top of a stack of linen shirts and scooped up the pile. *Home.* Even dogs had homes. Four walls, a bed, and a decent dinner. Maybe even a pat on the head every now and then.

He didn't want that. The feeling surged through him so suddenly and with such strength that he dropped the nest of shirts. The diary skittered across the planked floor with a soft hiss, landing just under the mattress. He dropped to his knees, reaching for it. The muscles of his arm screamed as he stretched. His mind joined in the wail.

He wanted to break the tether, snap the chain that tied him to his brother. He wanted to run, run free. *Why am I thinking this? What's happening to me?* Sweat beaded on his brow, fueled too by the heat of Benerict's look that he couldn't fully block out. Maybe this was the moment he was finally sober enough to remember the night, remember what he'd seen.

The mountain-man had spoken of the unfaithful. Laude wanted that. Maybe not in the way this city understood. No, he wanted it in the way he understood. His fingers curled around the diary.

"It'd be easy," Nathair was saying from across the bed. "In the chaos of battle, no one would know."

But when a dog ran wild and went feral, what did he find? Laude pulled the diary to his chest and curled his body around it. Would he wander long enough and lonely enough to come crawling back...or maybe fall into the grip of an even worse master? Would he end up like those on that pyre, his life snuffing away because he hadn't been strong enough to outrun the flames of others?

He didn't know but he had to try. He should try...he could. Maybe? The crown was Benerict's duty. Not his. He swallowed; his throat dry of anything but this singular desperation. Benerict would call it selfish.

"Do you want me to kill him for you?" Nathair was still talking. His rough voice dripped with something that could only be called vicious hunger. "I can do it. Kill the Godsent."

Laudilas felt his eyes squeeze shut. How far did one have to go to be free, how fast did they have to flee to outrun their own blood, their own world? His hands gripped the diary so tightly, some of the gilding from the back flaked into his palms.

Benerict didn't answer Nathair. *No blood. No bodies.* But Laude knew one thing as he pushed away from the golden morning light spilling across the floorboards and let himself sink into the shadows of the room—someday, someday, he would.

ELEVEN

DESMOND

Desmond last remembered collapsing face-first onto the bed. It was hours later when he awoke to sunlight stabbing his eyes and the inside face of his belt buckle making a semi-permanent tattoo on his torso. He sat up with a grunt that quickly turned to a groan. With a flop, he dropped back onto the pillows and buried his face.

He fumbled with the belt until it finally came loose, then with a blind heave, threw the blasted thing away from him. Its heavy buckle clattered against something solid before *thunking* softly onto a thick carpet.

Oh. Right. He was in his uncle's house. He pushed himself up on his elbows. On his uncle's bed.

That hadn't been his intention.

After leaving the palace sometime after midnight, he'd gone back to the embassy. He hadn't been sure what he would tell Artair. Whether he should apologize quietly or loudly shout that he'd been right, that he was always right. He was not and never had been the man for the job.

Artair wasn't a proud man. He would take the loss in stride—after sighing forlornly and gazing off into some far distance until Desmond felt like he'd just robbed a child of their chocolates.

But none of that had happened.

Desmond had walked through the embassy doors only to discover Artair was already gazing at something and it wasn't the distance.

"Des!" a warm, feminine voice had called out. Artair stood in the foyer wrapped in the tight, happy embrace of a woman. A woman dressed in the dark, suede garb of the Falcons' small but deadly archery force—Artair's petite raven-haired wife.

"Look what a ship from Vasili brought me." The count's wink was enough to tell Desmond that his friend's mind and interest was now far from books: lost, royal, or otherwise. *"No luck?"* he'd gone on to ask anyway with the barest of glances in his captain's direction.

Desmond had given a single shake of his head.

"Oh well." With a heave and a spin, Artair had his giggling wife in his arms, her arms around his neck, and was heading for the staircase. *"Tell me about it tomorrow. Maybe."*

That was when Desmond had decided to find other, less kiss-ambianced sleeping arrangements.

He barely remembered stumbling through the Thorne palazzo's front doors and making his way to the nearest chamber that had anything resembling a place he could prostrate every aching inch of himself.

It had to be near noon now. He sighed, roughing his hair with both hands. There was no use in even bothering Artair today.

Eira was a pretty woman, but she was not beautiful. But that wasn't why Artair loved her. She was honest and simple in a world filled with double dealings, fawning lords, and uncertain tomorrows. Her smile wasn't alluring like Isa's and there was no fire in her gaze like that periwinkle-eyed dancer. But still—

Desmond threw his legs over the edge of the bed. Visions of that slender dancer in her white and yellow costume had chased him like ghostly dandelion fluff all through the night. He would apologize to her if he could, for his foolish misunderstanding. *Chords though, so much spunk in such a small package. So much life.*

She may have cursed at him, but why did he feel like instead, she had cast out a line to a drowning man, or breathed a spark of white hope into a world blackened by every shade of darkness? His lips melted into something like a smile. Maybe he could find her again.

He scraped a hand through his hair one final time, shaking his head. Staggering to his feet, he started moving towards the tub. Someone had apparently filled it while he was sleeping. Lavender scented soap foamed over the top of the water like meringue on a pie. *What are they trying to imply?*

He shrugged out of his clothing piece by piece. The tub was a gargantuan carved affair sitting atop four stairs like a throne that overlooked the canal. *Barbarians.* With a sharp intake of air, he slid beneath the water. It wasn't hot, but still, warm enough. Behind his closed eyes, all he could see were hers. He pursed his lips, letting out a stream of air. The bubbles jetted out to ruffle the soap-formed ones above. Hope was one thing. Practicality another. No, he would probably never see that dancer again.

The rest of the afternoon passed in a dull blur. The first lawyer to come calling quickly dashed Desmond's fragile hope that he was actually rid of his uncle's fortune.

"No," the man said in a tone flat and dry as a duneless desert. "The account in the bank on dell'Oro was from horse race winnings. A pittance really in the grand scheme of things." He then went on to draw a large white handkerchief across his nose so slowly, Desmond had to keep blinking to assure himself time hadn't frozen still.

The second lawyer brought large white things as well, but fortunately, kept them away from his face. "This," he said, laying out a detailed sketch, "is the house here in the Masque. There is another"—a second sheet slid on top of the first—"in Prevecost. And last and definitely least, is this one in a village called—" The man screwed up his face in a way neither spectacles nor the restored eyes of youth could help. But Desmond barely noticed.

He snatched the smaller sheet from the man's hand. He could tell by the drawing that the place wasn't grand, more cottage than manor. It sat atop a hill with the barest hint of apple trees skimming the border of the paper. Something about the lines and angles of this one didn't say "house." They said a different word, one Desmond had not truly thought about since he was a boy.

Home.

"So." The questioning word snapped him from his reverie. "I'm to understand you are not interested in fully taking over your uncle's business ventures?" Cold eyes took in Desmond's Falcon leathers like a cat to a gutter rat. "I wouldn't worry if I were you. Both the house here and the one in Prevecost are maintained by excellent stewards who kept the master's affairs in impeccable order."

Desmond mentally snorted. He was in serious doubt of the "excellent" status of the steward here. He'd *yet* to meet the man. The one in Prevecost, he'd have to judge—someday.

The lawycr stood, scooping up the sketches. He didn't reach for the one in Desmond's hand and Desmond didn't offer it. He wasn't sure why.

He still wasn't sure why when the evening sun started tipping toward the horizon, its peach and orange light reflecting off the tea glass before him. He sat at a small table outside a café. The smell drifting out from the establishment's open windows promised seafood and pastries, all fried in too much butter.

It was quiet now. Not like the evening before when the city had seemed to heave, tearing at the bindings that tethered it to sanity. The sunset was calmer too, the blue sky soft with small clouds and waning light. Across the table, warm rays gilded the leaves and small blooms of a grotto of lemon trees.

There's gold on the leaves, but blood in the water. There's spring in the ground, but tears in the slaughter.

It was an old saying, one many loreborn recited at funerals or on first birthdays. Isa hadn't been wrong last night. Life *was* lived in dualities.

There's living and there's dying. There's hope and there's regret. There's all we long to remember and all we try to forget.

"Falcon!"

Desmond jumped. There was nothing graceful about it. If he'd been a cat, his tail would have flared like a chimney brush, evoking the laughter of every child in sight. But one looming man's chuckles were enough.

The Merced. *How.* What magic did this man possess that he'd managed to sneak up on Desmond twice now in under a day.

With one sweeping but precise movement, the man pushed the table's empty plate and half-full glass aside.

"I come bearing gifts," he said, not a little unlike an excited father on Coming Day. He set down a case. "Well, one gift anyway."

Desmond eased himself straighter, his hands flat on the table's top. He didn't know whether he should reach for a weapon or obey the encouraging jerk of the man's chin as he pushed the case closer.

It looked familiar. *What in the name of sense*—common or otherwise— Reaching out, he flipped up the two clasps in the center of the case and pushed back the lid.

Nestled inside just as it had been the night before was the Sagar violin. Desmond's eyes shot up to meet the Ansyran's. The man had dragged a small chair from a neighboring table and was helping himself to the remaining tea in the decanter. He smiled, wide and white toothed over the rim of a glass. "There's a note," he said, then went on to drain the glass dry.

So there was. Looped loosely inside the bow sat a narrow strip of paper. With the tug of a single finger, Desmond pulled it out. There was no salutation. Only one line, a dozen words plus two written in a tight, but well-practiced hand.

A single light can always be seen on a sea of darkness. Thank you. LD

But Desmond didn't need the signature, abbreviated though it was. The ink had been made with gold leaf. Only someone ridiculously royal or very bored—or both—would use something so lavish for such a short note.

His throat bobbed in an involuntary motion. The prince's smile last night had been *thank you* enough. Chords, the chance to rebel, to smack death in the face with a weapon—albeit one made of horsehair—had been more than sufficient.

"I—" he started, but the Ansyran cut him off with a raised hand.

"You'll play it well, yes, and cherish it?" His accent rolled with the question like a bottle bobbing through waves. "It was wasted on that minstrel anyway. He was willing to turn it over just for a ticket out of this city."

Desmond's open-mouthed expression morphed into a fast frown. *What about* my *money?*

The man seemed to read Desmond's unspoken growl. "Gambling debts. Drained your account to pay them off, but not enough to pay off blood debts, it seems." He shrugged. "Why do people get involved in the gangs," he muttered into his empty glass. "Anyway, he's free and the violin has a new home and my prince is only out the strength it took to stamp his seal on a set of travel papers."

Judging by the sudden tension in the man's brows, Desmond guessed expending energy was a greater show of gratitude for Luca Drake than any spending of coin.

Slowly, he settled the lid back over the violin. There was a question in the deliberateness of his movements. "So," he began.

"What do people call you when they don't want to use a title that's belonged to a hundred long-dead men?"

The tightness in the Merced's face melted into a smirk. "Is that a loreborn's way of asking a man his true name?" The other side of his lips turned up as well until his smile was broad again. "Polite but—how do you say it—busybodies; yes, that's what I've been told Albidonis are. They've got to know a thing, but they'll come up with the sugar-sweetest way of asking.

"My name"—he shifted in his seat, large arms locked against his chest—"is Nico, Nico of Tours. Tours," he went on as if Desmond somehow lived under a rock, "is where East meets West, heaven meets hell, and land and sea make love on sandy shores made of finest gold dust."

Ridiculous and romantic as it sounded, the last wasn't a lie. Ansyran sand was as valuable in some markets as gold and just as yellow. The first claim wasn't an extravagance either. Wedged between Vawdawr and the mid-Camrai Isles, Ansyra and its capital of Tours had always been pulled back and forth between the two greater kingdoms. Sometimes west towards the sunset. And at other times, the sunrise won, wooing the Ansyran people back towards the Camrai East.

Lately the Vawde had been winning, probably explaining why this man was here serving an imperial prince. But Desmond was curious.

"Why do you call him 'my prince'?" he asked. Was he really doing this? Showing interest in others again? *My prince.* There was a devotion in the way the man said it, something that burned deeper than the brand on his neck. Desmond had to know.

Nico's smile faded again, one eyebrow arching across his tan forehead. "You're observant," he said, in a quiet tone, unlike any of the ones he had used before. He looked at Desmond for a moment, blinking once, then twice, as if weighing something in a set of scales. "I will tell you, if a long tale is to your liking," he finally said. "It's not a good story, no, but it is about goodness, so listen well.

"When I was born," he began, settling back in his chair, "there were parents. When it became time for me to grow, there were none. But the streets become mother and father to many and brothers and sisters we become to each other. There was a girl who joined us one year. She was much younger than me. Beautiful, Falcon, as few have ever been. A flower, delicate and fair.

"But the fever came. Cobblestones may give you a resting place at night but they are not a good defense against sickness. Many died that year and many who lived were not the same. The girl, her mind went from sharp to simple, but her beauty remained.

"I did not desire her, but other men did. Last autumn, she vanished. Slavery is not a legal thing east of the Camrai, but it is still a done thing. I had not lived in Tours for some time, but when I returned, a friend told me that our little flower was gone. And that the ship that had stolen her bore the Drake crest.

"So, I came here. I would find her. And I would—" One large hand clenched into a fist so tight the knuckles cracked. Nico's eyes blazed and he swore something dark in a language Desmond had only the barest knowledge of.

"It's not hard to get into this palace. And it did not matter to me if I got out. Just as long as she did. Here, gossip is not cherished as simple stories as it is for your people. It's currency, a thing to barter and trade. But it only took a few broken noses for me to learn where she was and who had taken her. And *why.*

"I was told the second prince imperial had bought our flower as a gift for his youngest brother's nineteenth birthday. But it was all a joke. The youngest prince was a cripple and no man at all. Upon hearing that, I breathed in relief. At least for that night, I told myself, she was safe. But my hope snapped away with my informant's next words.

"'*The joke's on Prince Enzo,*' he said. '*I've been a servant in the court of physicians for many years and I've read all the notes. Prince Luca may be a broken horse who should have been put out of everyone's misery years ago, but he is not impotent.*' He smiled as if the twist amused him. '*Tomorrow, it will not be Enzo laughing.*'

"That's when I cracked his jaw. No one. No one would be laughing. And then I started running. Two—no—three guards met their end on the edge of my daggers before I reached Prince Luca's chambers. But when I arrived, what I saw was not what I had expected."

Nico's eyes drifted from the past to meet Desmond's. "No matter how much like a woman someone may look, if their mind is happier as a child, then let them be happy. And to my surprise that's what I saw.

"I entered an antechamber at first, one made of glass on three of its sides; even the ceiling was paned with the same. Trees lined the walls thick with branches, and over my head, ivy trailed down like ribbons. Some of what grew there I knew, but most was exotic, coming from lands most of us only dream of.

"And then there were the animals. A monkey, a few cages with birds, but most flew free around the room. And then—" He paused and smiled, lost again in memory. "There were the dogs. Young ones, old, big, small. And there, sitting surrounded by half a dozen white, yapping balls of fluff, I found our flower. Happy, laughing, a look on her face only innocence could bring.

"I did not speak to her or let her know I was there. I doubted she even understood the danger she could still be in. I went looking for that danger. But I found it sound asleep. Or so I thought.

"I'm a fighter. I've been one ever since the day I left my mother's womb weeks earlier than I should have. I know a man's breathing. When someone has told themselves 'no' and is reminding themselves of it again and again.

"I found His Highness on a low couch with his back to the door of the glass room. He lay curled around himself, fist against his heart, like a man wounded. His eyes were closed, but in every measured breath I heard it. He would not touch her; it was not an option. But he was human, hurting, alone. If any man had an excuse that could be brushed away by pity, even I might have admitted, he did. It was not an easy 'no.'"

Nico fixed his gaze on Desmond like a leveled sword. "I wanted to know why." He shook his head. "Not like you want to know why. Not because I was curious or bored or looking for yet another page in a new book. Men in this city, in that family, they take. Death takes. Power takes. It does not give.

"But *this*? That was giving. Do you see that frog?" His chin suddenly jerked to the lip of a fountain bubbling about a dozen paces away.

Desmond blinked at the abrupt change of subject but turned to look.

"I fished that slimy beast out of the bottom of a back canal yesterday. My prince saw it fall from a lily pad. Dead as last millennium's bones I said it was, but he didn't believe me. He was right: even near-dead things can sometimes be saved." Nico sighed, folding his large, scarred hands on the top of the table.

"He saved our little flower and he saved me. I'm tied to imperial service for life in payment for those guards I killed. I could run—" He shrugged. "But I stay to see what happens. For some reason, I feel like...like my life depends on it." His eyes narrowed, somehow fixed on nothing and yet everything at once. "I think—" His tone suddenly dropped so only Desmond could hear. "I think next, he means to save this city."

"He wants to become imperator?" It was the first time he'd spoken since the story began and Desmond knew he sounded surprised, his tone too loud, as if a soldier like himself didn't believe a cripple could claim a crown. But he well knew cunning often cut deeper than tempered steel.

It was just—the boy's face had looked so young. His emotions so many. He was someone a soldier should protect, not someone whose banner might be used by others as a shield from the darkness.

"I said save it." Nico's abrupt words and snort interrupted his thoughts. "Not drive both him and it to bloody insanity."

Desmond's brows twisted in a frown. There was probably a layered meaning to those words, but it sounded complicated, like a weaver's stitch beyond his knowledge or ability. He sighed.

"Your people," Nico said after a moment's silence. "From what I've seen with this whole dance over the diary, they like freedom? Do they like it more than stories?"

Once again, the man was changing the subject. Desmond settled his shoulders back against the chair. It was fair, he supposed. He had asked questions, now it was his turn to give answers.

But what answer? He sifted the Ansyran's words through his mind. Whatever interest he'd had in the imperial schemes of the young Drake were cut off, directed back to more personal, more pressing issues.

The glass crown. He'd let them win last night. Queen Adile's diary was just that, a book filled with old memories. There was nothing magical or really even sacred about it. Other royal artifacts remained, too. He stretched out his legs and let them fall into a cross at his ankles. A thin trace of dust gilded the narrow stitching that ran in a straight line down the center of both boots. One line. Two sides. Rebels and royals.

Just like the dust would brush away with one swipe of a cloth, so the tenuous peace in Albidon might vanish someday too. *As long as it's not directly the result of last night. My violin playing won't stand up to the insult.*

"My people don't want hope, Merced," he finally said. "They want to be happy. Freedom makes them happy." He shrugged, the leather of his vest squeaking a little at the movement. There was nothing romantic about the loreborn's desire to escape oppression. It was just life, plain and simple.

"Ah." Nico looked strangely disappointed. "So, just for themselves the nightingale flies, then?"

The what? Desmond wasn't sure what the expression on his face looked like but his mind had gone flat with utter bewilderment.

Nico coughed. "I read through the royal diary a little." He looked abashed, an odd look for his rugged face. "It spoke of a little bird that sings unseen in the night, soothing hearts and inspiring minds. A promise that even in darkness there is life. Its symbol, it was etched on the back of the book. I thought maybe—birds fly far, you know."

Desmond eased himself straighter in his chair, hands braced on his elbows. He knew the story of the nightingale. Everybody did. Rebels used to scratch little birds on barn doors or hitching posts during the royal overthrow as a sign of a safe meeting place. But it was just a thing for commoners and dreamers, a loreborn thing.

It had no place here with princes and empires. He gave Nico a studying look. Whatever imperial ambition, no matter how benevolent, Luca had, no loreborn fairytale was coming to help. Oil and water did not mix. And neither did dragons and gales. But there was no use saying all this. He let his muscles relax again. It had been a long twenty-four hours. Maybe the Ansyran had just gotten a little swept away in the drama of it all.

"Do you want me to write out the music to what I played last night for His Highness?" he said instead. "He would have it then if he wanted to hear it again. I think I could score it to be played by the harp as well." If he couldn't give answers or assurances to whatever the Merced was poking at, he could at least give this.

Nico seemed to consider the proposal for a moment. "No," he said slowly, standing to his feet. "No." This time with more conviction. "Life can't be written down. It's no great sorrow if a thing isn't trapped in ink. It was lived. It's in the soul then. Forever." He tapped his chest.

"I wish you all the luck though," he went on, tone rippling with energy again, whatever odd disappointment gone from his face. "I hear you've entered into a king's ransom in gold." His smile tightened. "The war will be long, and if you survive it, life will be longer. You never know when it might just be your salvation."

Desmond snorted but said nothing. He didn't want to know how deep the hell would have to be for that inheritance to be any sort of saving grace. But...the man was right. Money had its merits. He just hoped it would be a long time before he ever had to discover any of them.

"Ah, I have one more thing for you." Nico turned back to the table and *thumped* the edge of it with one thick finger. "I'm told at least one of your stories walks. The Immortal Chronicler?"

Desmond sat up straight, the legs of his chair scraping against the brick.

Nico laughed, white teeth flashing in the waning light. "Stories will be the death of you, Falcon. Anyway, he's down by the docks telling his tales. I'm not sure exactly where but if you can find him, it might be fun." Then with a wink the man was gone.

Desmond watched as he stopped by the fountain, scooping up the frog that still sat on its edge. He set it on his shoulder, then, step by step, faded from sight.

A gush of warm light spilled across the table. Desmond looked up to see the owner of the café standing on a ladder, small torch in hand. One by one, the woman set to lighting a trio of open-faced lanterns. That reminded him. Reaching inside his vest, he felt for his money pouch.

Instead, his fingers curled around the small note that Luca had written. He didn't remember putting it there, but there it was nestled against the sketch of the cottage he was still carrying. He pulled it out.

A single light can always be seen—

He sighed, his breath pulling in slowly and slipping away even slower. Man was not made to know the future. And he could not undo his past, maybe not even his present, not fully anyway. But—there were things he could do.

Resting his head back against the top of the chair, Desmond looked at the sky. If the Chronicler truly was immortal, he could wait, just a few minutes. The sun had set now, the east melting from blue to shadow, the west still rimmed with light.

There is light and there is shadow, the old saying said as it finished. *There is good and there is not. There's summer and there's winter. There's hurt—*

But always, always, there is God.

TWELVE

KENNET

It had been a long time since he'd told the story, here in this place where the gulls blew in from the bay and peddlers hawked their wares. Where children danced over crates and old men sat watching and laughing, resting their bones on the sun-baked stones.

There was no explosion of light, no dancing of shadows upon the waters as he began. But still, the story rang out. It was an old story—some might even say, the very oldest tale of all.

They say that in the beginning there was light and there was darkness and there was man. But man loved the darkness more than the light and chose therein to dwell. The world became black and the hearts of men blacker still. There was no beauty, only tears and sorrow and death.

But the light did not forget man, for the Light had made man and he loved him with an everlasting love. In the fullness of time, as a midwinter's sun slipped away from the chill kiss of the stars, he came down and walked among men once more. With his coming, light poured into the darkness. It did not quail before the Great Dark but grew and spread until it touched every place and every man.

Then there was a day when the story added a new chapter. Alone on a great hill, Light and Darkness met, and there they waged the greatest battle of their eternal war. Creation drew in its breath, and the winds stood still in their eternal dance.

Time herself paused, hands frozen in place. All eyes watched every sword stroke and every blow. At long last, they thought, the Darkness would be defeated forever and Light would reign over the earth once more.

But no, the Light did not prevail; his radiance and beauty were snuffed out and trampled underfoot by the Great Prince of Darkness.

Death had won.

The world faded into blackness once more. Shadows returned and dark dreams slipped their way back into the minds of men. The wise men of that age laid down their pens and shut the book. The story had ended.

Or so they thought. Maybe they were justified in their thinking, or maybe they simply were not as wise as they had wanted others to think.

They did not understand that only by death can Death be undone. Only by the giving of Life's blood can life return. And so it was that the Light had laid down his life in darkness that those held captive by the Dark might rise again to life anew.

In the silence, Time began to tick once more, and the winds rejoined hands to dance and whisper of what they had seen and what they knew. The sun sighed and bowed his crimson head over the world, then slipped away. The stars came out and sang songs of mysteries that had been and the ones still yet to come. The next day the sun returned, and then, in the evening, the stars came, and then another day.

But on the third day, just as the stars sang their final song and the curtains drew closed for the entrance of the sun, another light lit the horizon. It started as a simple flicker but as each moment passed, its brilliance grew and spread until once again it had touched every place and every man.

For this too the wise had not understood. Death cannot keep Eternity; the Dark cannot truly destroy that which has never been sullied by his sin-blackened hands. And so, the Light returned and this time, he made a promise to man, a promise that he would never leave and that the light would never fade.

Life and Death, Light and Darkness. They were a choice now, one every man must make. Some ran from the Light for it showed the truth and darkness of their deeds, but others came to the Light, and there they found life and rest and hope.

In time, that age passed from the world, but the story itself did not end. It went on.

And I say that it goes on still. For though it is a story, like so many others, some stories are true. And this, this is the Great Story, and we are each one of us a part of its telling.

For the wages of sin is death; but the gift of God is eternal life through Jesus Christ our Lord. Romans 6:23

EPILOGUE

Stones

Religion. It was what was wrong with the world. The stones had been sure of this for centuries beyond recount. Ever since the day they'd tasted the Chronicler's blood and every man since who'd died for believing what he wanted and not what he was told.

All day long, the citizens of the Masque had buried bodies and tossed ashes out to hungry waves. Sealed side by side, as silent sentries, the lighthouse stones had watched. It was eventide now. The sun's warmth on their grey faces was draining away, overlaid by the cold hand of night.

But nothing was as cold as death. She was here; the stones could see her jagged silhouette threading through the few mourners who remained on the beach. No one saw her. No one ever saw the Dark Sister, but all men felt her touch, eventually. Her smile was curved like a scythe, her footsteps measured as if she were counting—bodies maybe? Or the steps of a dance.

She did not stop until she reached the final figure on the beach. A young woman knelt in the sand beside the shrouded body of what must have been a child. The little one's death had not been natural if the dried blood staining the cloth was any indication. The stones could not see the young woman's face, cloaked as it was by a river of golden hair. But she was crying, the shivering shake of her shoulders bending her low.

Death laughed, a sound skull-hollow but vicious all the same. "Foolish. Foolish," she rasped to the young woman. "Every year, every day, every second, it's the same. Men were made to die, but still, you mourn them."

The young woman lifted her head. The stones expected to see tears swimming in her eyes. But the instant they met Death's, their soft golden hue blazed hot like sand in a desert storm. She stood. Unfolded, she towered over Death but her frame was reed-like and frail. "Man was made to *live*," she said, hands clenching at her sides.

The stones strained in their mortar-made prison. The woman's voice was so soft, slipping through the air like the hiss of an hourglass.

Death laughed again. "And yet time and time again, they choose the things that lead them to me. Just like *time and time again*"—she huffed as if the phrase amused her—"they waste you, ignore you, think you're infinite to them, always more, always another day, another heartbeat. Man is *misery*. Why do you care? *Why?*"

The golden woman didn't answer, her hair slipping down to cover her face once again. Death stamped her foot. But the sand beneath her feet did not bow to her fury. She kicked at it. Still nothing.

"I always win," she snarled anyway. "And most of all, in all this world, I win on the day that was yesterday. Some of them die because of folly, some because of sin. And some—" A hand flung out to point towards the dark waves. "Some are turned into the dust from which they were made just for saying 'no' to someone just as human as they are. So many reasons in one day. So many come to me. In one year less a day, it will come again. I always win," she repeated, grinding her heel. "Nothing, *no one* will change this."

The sand beneath Death's feet remained still and so did the woman before her. With a final huff, the Dark Sister faded into the shadowy night.

But the young woman remained. Gently, she lifted the child, a hand stopping for a moment where the bloodstain was turning to a muddy brown. A blow from a drunken parent, a fall from too great a height, a little one in the wrong place at the wrong time? Who knew how this life had come to end.

"Ashes to ashes, dust to dust," she whispered, wading out into the tide and setting the body to drift in the embrace of a wave. "Loved are the living. Beloved were the dead. This has God promised. This hath he said."

Turning back to the beach, she pulled herself from the water, the linen fabric of her sodden dress heavy around her legs. In the twilight, the stones could not tell what color the garment was. But it looked new and somehow ancient—no, primordial—at the same time.

Time and time again...

The woman collapsed back onto her knees, palms against the ground, and then, she screamed. Hands plunging deep into the sand, Time's wail ripped the air. The stones shuddered as the sound shot through them. Three centuries they had stood here on this shore. Three hundred holidays. Countless lives. And every year, Time had come.

She was not Wisdom, and she was not Patience. She was every heartbeat cut off too soon. Every life ruined by hatred, pride, or jealousy. She was every hourglass-sand man had ever wasted. Tonight, as the moon rode through a cloudless sky and the tide retreated back into the sea, the sand was wet with the tears of every hope ever lost.

The stones wanted to reach out. Over the centuries, a few had wiggled loose, hoping to comfort Time when the day came. But they'd been taken away or swept out to sea too soon. Just as the sun blazed in victory over night every dawn and sank in bloody loss every sunset over and over again, so the stones had stopped hoping this scene would ever change. That hope would ever come.

The shadows had whispered of change the other night. The waters had passed news of happenings in the city from wave to wave until even the shore had heard the tales.

But stone was hard. Stone only made things when there was order, structure. And in this place, sad as it was, this was the order of things. What they had seen, the stones would see again and again until mortar failed and wind won, and each fell forever into the sea.

"You're wrong." Time's sand-soft voice jolted the stones from their dark reverie. She had pulled her hands from the ground. With one, she wiped the tears from her face, leaving trails of golden sand across her cheeks. The other she set against a single stone nestled in the base of the lighthouse.

Her delicate mouth puckered into a small smile. "You don't believe me," she said. "It's all right to mourn, but— Hmm, maybe I should show you." With a yank, the stone came loose. It winced in the surprising strength of her grasp.

But so warm, it thought. *So alive.*

She pulled it up until it was level with her golden gaze. The stone glanced down. In Time's other hand was a fistful of sand. "Forgive me," she said barely above a whisper. "But you will see."

In an instant, in one solitary flex, a crushing, searing pain ripped the stone from top to bottom, grain from grain, until it was a fine powder, a thousand bits of dust, nothing more. Into the air it flew just as Time's other hand rose as well, flinging up the sand that she had held there.

Around the crushed, flying stone, the sand danced, a thousand heartbeats, a million moments yet to live. "This," Time cried, letting her voice ring out like the call of the hour from a symphony of bells, "is the future. These are the choices. *This* is the hope."

The wind swept into the dance, swirling the flying grains higher into the air. The moon mixed in its light, and there in the glowing beams, the stone saw images begin to effervesce.

The first one reflected last night's gossip from the waters, that of the Knight and the Dancer. Their paths would meet again, two threads becoming one, a shimmering strand of red. Sometimes the petals of freshest Coming roses lined the way, and other times, it was the stain of life's precious blood.

The image shifted, and against Time's golden sand, the Godsent rose like a cloudless sunrise. But then, just as his glowing orb cleared the horizon, the light snuffed out. The stone gasped, shielding its face as the wind turned hard, blowing fierce in a gale made of Greed, Shadows, and crawling Nightmares. *No, no,* it thought. *The light was so warm, so good. What hope is this— Ouch!*

The stone darted away as something small and shattered, just like itself, began to dance beside it. The stone opened its eyes to see sparks, splintered bits of sunrise. The sparks joined hand in hand against the gale until a wildfire blazed, its heat casting the world in a fierce, golden light. In that glow, the dark dreams faded and dawn was lit once more.

The winds dipped, bowing to the strength of the rising light and shifted south, threading new images from the sand. The stone watched in wonder. The Immortal had not been wrong. The White and Red Dragons would rise. And they would battle. But into their fight came another, a winged viper, the smallest of flaming beasts. Driven by the blast of Winter's Bane, she rose above her greater siblings and by White's side, she fought.

But before the stone could see their end, the wind suddenly calmed, dropping to a gentle cadence, the moonlight darting behind a cloud.

Wait! it cried, turning to look at Time, now far below. *The hope!*

Time smiled. "Shhh. Look." With one finger, she pointed to a spot, so small the stone had not seen it. But there, soaring over them all, was something else—someone else. Known and yet unknown, he wore ten thousand faces and only one. Time smiled again, a thing both wonderful and wild to behold.

"Beware," her voice echoed out. All that was and all that could be swirling around her in a symphony of heartbeats. The sight and sound of promise. Of hope. "Beware, City of Bones—Beware the Nightingale!"

AFTERWORD

- Laudilas & Co. will return in the SPECTRUM DUOLOGY.
- Luca will return after in the SAINTS & SINNERS SERIES.
- To discover if Desmond and the Dancer ever meet again, keep reading this book.

BONUS CONTENT

Dawnsong

Did Desmond and the Dancer ever meet again? Find out next in *Dawnsong*, a novellette set two years after *Illuminare*.

BRYN SHUTT
DAWNSONG

www.brynshutt.com

Cover art by Hannah Rogers

Illustrations by Irina Plachkova

Edits by Deborah O'Carroll

PRAISE FOR DAWNSONG

Delightfully promising and packed with unexpected depth, this fantasy adventure was satisfying on its own while leaving me wanting more from this fantasy world. Go read it. It's sure to please. *~Sarah K. L. Wilson, USA Today bestselling author*

Lyrical and poignant, Dawnsong is a brilliant introduction to a brand new world, and full of timely reminders to open our eyes and live. *~C.M. Banschbach, author of* The Dragon Keep Chronicles

Dawnsong is a sweet, slow-burn, character-driven story that delivers a vivid world and promises even more for the next installment. I've always loved the snippets I see of this world, and this one is no exception. Eager for the next! *~CS Johnson, award winning author*

For Barbara. This story is for you. It's also your fault, but in all the most wonderful ways.

"Everyone thinks of changing the world, but no one thinks of changing himself." Leo Tolstoy

ONE

Prevecost, Albidon
2nd of Syl, 1021 A.R.

The rain fell the only way it ever did. Down. It rattled against roof tiles, splashed onto street cobbles and streamed along with tears down the face of the young guard. But Lilias Khove doubted she was the only one in Prevecost crying tonight.

It had been three months since shadowpox had come. The disease had spread through Albidon like water gushing over a broken dam, sweeping away both old and young alike. So far, Lilias had lost four friends, all dancers in the same company she had once called home. Playhouses had shut their doors. The rest of the company had disbanded, seeking country homes or employment beyond the now empty theatre halls.

Tonight, as she walked her beat through Rue de Sasson, a small part of Lilias wished her own reason for losing her position had been as simple as that. Something that didn't wag the fingers of failure straight at her.

But a dancer is strong, agile and quick. It had been easy to find employment in the city guard seven months ago. And now, especially on nights like this, it was hard to imagine she had ever been anything else.

With an irritated grunt, she scrubbed her knuckles over her face, pushing the water and—for now—the memories away.

"Life's tough, then it's over, girl," her babka had always said.

Lilias hadn't believed her; she still didn't...maybe.

Reaching in her pocket, she started fishing for the salmon-stuffed pancakes she'd squirreled away there. She'd made them on her own. Street vendors in the night markets were rare now. One had to fend for oneself—even if that fending in her case had meant three scorched skillets and a garret flat full of smoke. The pancakes *had* looked good. Taste would be another—

"You! Stop, thief!" The call was muffled, at least two miles away. But in a city locked up and silent as the death it feared, sounds were precious few. And this one was punctuated by a shrill scream.

Lilias' hand jerked from her pocket and up to her belt in an instant, pulling lose the little silven lamp that hung there. Its cool, golden glow bloomed to full strength with a tap of her fingers against the globe. The streetlamps in the city hadn't been lit in weeks. Not since every household kissed by one nightwatchman's flames had all died of the sickness in Falcon's Roost. Light created shadows. Better to die in the dark.

The cry hadn't come from straight ahead. It had been east, near the waterside. "Chords," she groaned and started to run.

Her beat was usually a peaceful one. Up Rue de Sasson, past the printers' guild and straight on to Devran Square. A statue stood in the square's center, a memorial to the Immortal

Chronicler. Why a man supposedly still alive after one thousand years needed a memorial no one had ever been able to rationally explain to her, but she liked looking up into the grave face in the statue. It felt like a promise that someone, somewhere was remembering all their stories, penning them down for generations to come.

She'd told the statue her story one night with a mouth stuffed with lemon cake. If bronze could look bored, it had.

"Khove! Is that you? Khove!" At the corner of Merri and Thyme, another silven lamp flickered in the corner of Lilias' eye. Lucky stars, she wasn't alone. Her pace slowed as the light came closer. She recognized the guard: Deods, an older man from the southern fens judging by his accent.

"Did you hear that?" he puffed, his breath frosting in the Syl night air like wispy clouds.

"I think it came from Dockside, by the warehouse, you know." She bent, clasping her knees and breathing in and out hard for a moment herself. "The one that stores all those barrels of ink. I think it came from there."

"Ah." The word came out harsh and short, like it was an answer all to itself. "That's Jay territory, leave it be. Leave it be." The man clipped his light back onto his belt and shook his head, but to Lilias he looked nothing but relieved.

The Jays were a gang. Everyone knew that. But they weren't dangerous, at least not that Lilias had ever heard. They were made up mostly of the children of sailors, both true born and bastard. Their fathers protected the seas, they claimed, and they the shore. They shielded the innocent from vice, guarded the pockets of merchants from pirates and saw to it that only the finest cider was served in Dockside's taverns.

But mostly, they were just dockrunners. How much of everything else was real, who knew. But it was the legend of the thing that mattered. Every port city knew of the Jays of Prevecost.

"City watch doesn't have jurisdiction in Dockside." The man's voice broke into Lilias' thoughts. "Their own rules; their own justice."

"But—"

He waved her off, already starting to walk away. "You'll learn, little lady."

"But—" It had sounded like a child's scream. A small child. Lilias pulled her light against her chest as the other guard continued to fade from view. Dockside was always alive, no matter the time of day; even with the plague, that part of the city had still seemed to silently buzz. She'd never thought about who patrolled the streets and alleys down there. She had just assumed it had been someone. Someone *not* a child. Someone not waiting for a da to come home riding the four winds.

But tonight, the vibe echoing up to where she stood was stillness. So still. Like an empty theatre hall, holding phantom shadows of what had been. Like something that suddenly realized it was dying...

The scream came again.

"Tainted take it." She flung the light out in front of her and took off again. Whatever arrangement the city had with its seafarer offspring wasn't worth leaving a little one crying in the night.

What could it cost her? A lost job? She already had experience there.

The smell of the docks was always a sudden thing. You didn't think Prevecost was so close to the sea, but then suddenly, you and your nose were there. The scents hit Lilias in the same instant fingers latched onto her belt.

"Oi!" She swerved to the side, her shoulder slamming into a mossy stone wall, but the fingers' grip was strong. She felt a tug. *Her money pouch.* For a moment, her mind slid back to her old life: a pretty, well paid dancer with fine clothes and a heavy purse. *Help!* The word almost flew out of her mouth. But wait, no, she was the help now, her finery locked away in a trunk. The only thing in the leather pouch that looped over her belt was a rusted iron key. Guard pay was late on chronic levels.

"Let go! I don't have anything." She grabbed the fingers with her free hand and tried to pry them away. They were cold, so cold and small and... She dropped her other arm, letting her light illuminate the fingers and then a face. A child. A girl no more than nine in a tattered coat that might have fit two winters ago but not now. Owlish eyes ringed with black came into focus for a heartbeat, then they jerked away from the light's golden glare.

"You caught me! You caught me. I won't run. I swear!"

"What?"

"I won't run, dimilessa, just cuff me; I'll go quiet, I will!" There was desperation in that voice.

"What on earth? I'm not going to arrest you." Lilias grabbed for the child's hand as the fingers finally pulled away.

"But I tried to steal?" The child's tone had pitched up to a soft wail now. Something wasn't right. Lilias felt unease prickle down her spine.

"Just don't do it again. It's okay." She tried to sound soothing, but she also didn't have time for this. "Now, tell me, did you hear a scream earlier? It came from near—wait, right about—was it you? Did you try to steal from someone else? Where are they?"

"Yes?" That was a lie. The answer trembled; it felt like a question of its own.

What the chords-blasted? Lilias took in her surroundings. It was the old ink warehouse just like she thought. Faint scuffles sounded from behind the wall opposite her. Too large to be rats. But human? Bending down, she hefted the small girl onto a stack of crates.

"Explain."

"Well, I..." the girl started then hiccupped, drawing a thin hand across her eyes. "I thought if I screamed loud enough, a guard from uppards might come. If I pinched something straight from them—I wouldn't have kept it, dimi, I promise. I just thought, I mean. If I got arrested, you stay for all day and night, yes?" She made a looping swirl with her hand like the cycle of the sun.

"Yes?" Lilias had no idea where this was going. Her arms were folded so tightly, the leather of her vest was creaking quietly in protest.

"They feed you in jail. Jeri told me so. He got locked up for shoving some foreign squire. Got locked up for three days. Said it was the best eating he had since the plague came. It was just for the eating, dimi; I would have given your pouch back, promise."

Lilias blinked. The rain wasn't falling here. The slanted, crooked roofs were too close together. She blinked again, but water still pooled in her eyes. "You wanted to get arrested..." the words trailed off. "So you could get something to eat?"

The girl sniffed. "I thought it wasn't a bad idea." She shrugged, her little shoulders rising and falling. "You did come."

Lilias had come, running through dark streets when she'd no legal obligation. Why? The primal, practical sense that children shouldn't cry in the night? She blinked again. This time the tears splashed away down her cheeks, clearing her vision. The only light in the narrow street was the one coming from the silven lamp still clenched in her hand. But she could see the walls, the dead leaves littering the damp-slick cobbles, the little girl still perched on the crate. Automatically, Lilias reached into her pocket and extended her food without a word.

The dark street came alive. What had been an empty, narrow pathway containing only two people suddenly became packed with at least half a dozen. Children of all shapes and sizes emerged from the doors of the warehouse and swamped the crate and its little occupant. The girl jumped to her feet and thrust Lilias' supper into the air. "Get in a line, seriously," she said. "I'll divvy it up, promise!"

Lilias found herself jostled backwards until she was pinned against the opposing wall. But even if she hadn't been, she wouldn't have been able to move. All the air had left her lungs. This wasn't happening. Not in neat, proper Prevecost. Lilias had traveled all seven kingdoms in her four years as a dancer with the Troupe Beli. She'd seen rich and she'd seen poor. But Albidon—home—had always been different. But this, children trying to get themselves cuffed and hauled away, with black marks next to their names for any potential employer to see just for something in their belly...practical wouldn't fix this.

"I don't understand," she heard herself saying over the murmur of voices. "You're Jays, aren't you? I thought you worked the docks?" A host of wide eyes turned almost in unison to look at her.

"No pay, dimi. No ships unloading. No pay; no food."

"But—" Lilias raked her fingers through her hair, pulling strands loose from her braid. "Isn't there some Jay code that keeps you fed anyway?" The host of eyes looked at her like she was auditioning for Madman Number One.

"No pay; no food," a boy simply repeated, shoving his little, one-bite sized portion into his mouth. He shrugged and gave no further explanation.

"You were all waiting then?" Lilias turned her questions back to the girl.

She nodded. "Maybe more than one person would come." She shrugged. "Or at least the others could see how it was done. I know the guards don't usually come down here, but it was worth a try."

Such desperation. *Oh, chords, this is not happening and it definitely is not happening to me.* "So, let me get this straight. Ships aren't unloading, so you have no work which means you have no pay, and therefore, no food? Yeah?"

Half a dozen nods blinked at her in the darkness.

Her knees weakened until she found herself slumping onto a mossy stone step behind her. Inside, her stomach started to turn.

"How many are you?" she finally sputtered.

"The older ones say they're going to board the ships and raid them, but we're too little to go, so we won't get any of it. Not if we didn't help. There's three and a score of us. Just six here, though."

Lilias wasn't sure who the speaker was, maybe it was the boy from earlier. So, twenty-three tykes with stomachs emptier than a kingless crown. She forced herself to take in the scene before her again.

You're a proud woman, Khove, her dancing master had once said. *You think only of yourself and the rules. You must* see *others to truly be a dancer. It's not enough to just know the steps and be good at them; you must watch others: your partners, your musicians, your audience. Give and take. You must be willing to look into another's eyes and let them look into yours. Dancing is more than the motions. You must see, Khove, open your eyes and see beyond yourself. That is how you create true art. Seeing is how—*

The words replayed as she took in each face. Some looked at her gratefully, but life had flushed hope down a muddy drain long ago. But some—the little girl who'd tried to take her pouch—there was still hope there. "You did come," she'd said. But anyone would have come. That was the right thing, the practical, expected thing decent people did. It was the steps of a dance as found in a manual. But staying? That wasn't just the motions. That was something else...

She could go to the dockmaster; demand something be done? Maybe. Go to the captain of the city guard? No. They didn't bother with the docks, apparently. The Unmaker? Yesterday afternoon's broadsheets had said he was in the city. *Pffi, a man who threw a king off his throne isn't worried about two dozen or so children*, she reminded herself. Besides, yelling and pleading with authorities took time; getting them to listen took miracles. These children didn't have time for either.

Some inborn habit sent her reaching once more for her money pouch. Money would fix this—for tonight at least. There were still enough shops who would open if the knocking came with the jingle of coins. But she had nothing. Nothing but that darn key.

Scrubbing a hand through her hair again, her mind let out a moan. *Oh, Jesu, what do I do? All I've got is—*

That darn key. That key she kept as a keepsake to remember Da. That darn key that led to—

"Wait a minute." She found herself speaking and standing all in a jumbled rush. "Who knows where Rue Mahi is?"

There was silence for a moment, but then one little voice from the back piped up, "It's at the edge, near An Gragan, dimi. It's spooky out there."

"Pffi, nonsense." But the little one wasn't wrong. The half-submerged bogland that housed an even more than half-crumbling lighthouse was shrouded so often in mists, few could ever even have claimed to have seen it. But she had. Her smuggler father had seen to that.

"Go to Mahi, all the way to the end. With this key." She reached her hand out to the thief girl. "Open the red painted door in the wall. It will take you into the Under."

She hadn't thought it was possible for these children's eyes to get any wider. More than a few gasps echoed up at her.

"The Under ain't real, dimi. That door just leads to some old cellar."

"That's what royalists want you to think," Lilias muttered under her breath.

"No, it will take you under the water. It's safe, I promise. At the end, use the same key. It will open into the lighthouse. There's food stored there. Nothing fresh, but it will keep you full for a while. I promise—" Promise what? "I promise, I'll do something. I have to go." She cast a nervous glance over her shoulder. The sound of loud shouts was starting to spill out from a tavern door less than a dozen feet away. She was too rattled now to learn just how far "their own rules, their own justice" would go. Her uniform suddenly felt like a loud banner of rebellion.

"Go on." She gave the key a shake and felt a sweep of relief when the young girl took it. Already, the others were starting to melt out of view. But the girl jumped down from her crate.

"Thank you, dimi," she said, wrapping her arms around Lilias' waist and squeezing with surprising strength. "Thank you for seeing us. People never do, you know. Nobody sees you down here."

The burning in Lilias' eyes ignited with fresh tears. Bending down, she pulled the girl in tight.

"Why is that? Is it all the exotic coming off the ships? How busy everyone is? Why does no one see?"

I will give you anything, anything but myself.

Those words, from an old Varr play, words of a faithless lover, words Lilias had thrown back at her dancing master, echoed now in her head. She'd interrupted his speech that day. He'd had one more thing to say. Something she didn't want to hear. It was that something beyond "practical," beyond the motions.

"We don't know how to live." Lilias whispered these words into the little girl's hair before finally pushing her away. She doubted the girl heard them. They weren't meant for her anyway. Lilias watched the slender form disappear into the dark wet.

That is how you create true art. Seeing is how you begin to truly live. That's what the dancing master had tried to say to her unlistening ears.

Lilias turned and started to make her way step by step back towards the lightless streets and plague-shuttered houses, everything still as silent as the death it feared. *Why is it*, she wondered, the thought settling like a prickling burr into her mind as she clipped her light back onto her belt. *Why are we so afraid of dying when we've never even tried to live?*

PhantomRin.

TWO

Dawn was starting to streak through the clouds as she emerged back onto Rue de Sasson. The High Sanct bells had already begun sounding out the sixth hour, the end of her shift. Lilias made her way through the quiet streets toward the guardhouse of District Three. There she'd lock up her dagger and short sword, check for pay that was certain not to be there and go home.

Home. It was a strange word for a dancer to think on, really. Home for so many years had been one theatre house or another, ships, caravans, anything that could take her from one performance to the next. The little garret flat she currently labeled as her address sat at the top of a Vawde bakery. The only real perk of living there was first dibs on day-old pastries. But it wasn't home, not really. None of it had ever been. The word in its truest form was like a star, something beautiful, but always out of reach.

She let out a sigh and rolled her shoulders. *Just one more street.*

Prevecost was made of four districts, all built up from odd angles and lines, like the architect who had designed the city had been riding a bucking stallion when he'd sketched out the plans. District Three encompassed most of Prevecost's commercial center, with its granite banks, emerald slated guild houses and massive library. The Great Tome House was said to hold more books, scrolls and manuscripts than all the other libraries of the world combined.

It was a fitting thing, most supposed, considering Albidon's chief revenue came from stories, both ones they'd created over the centuries—and the ones they'd stolen. The library itself covered an entire city block, but tucked into the eastern edge of the structure was a three-story wattle and daub afterthought of a building, the guardhouse of District Three. No one knew why custom dictated that it have exactly fourteen holding cells and house the high captain's headquarters, but it did.

"Khove! Oh, chords, there you are." Lilias hadn't made it four steps into the building when her shoulders were grabbed, and she found herself being pulled into a side room.

"Tainted take it," she snarled without bothering to see who her assailant was.

"The Unmaker's carriage was waylaid tonight!"

With a hard twist, Lilias finally managed to untangle her arm and face the voice babbling in her ear. It was Juli, a veteran guard who'd seen at least seven years in the watch.

"What?"

"Yes! And it's your fault! They want you upstairs." Juli gave her a push and a look that said, "I have never been happier to be me and not you."

"What?" Lilias repeated the words again, squeezing her eyes shut then reopening them, hoping, in vain, for a saner world to come into view.

"You didn't finish your beat. The Scarlet Hand was waiting for the Unmaker in Devran Square. You weren't there to sound the alarm. Deods said you went running off to the docks over some yelling or something."

Oh. Oh. Chords in flats and sharps. Shoving past Juli, Lilias made it to the landing that led to the second floor of the guardhouse in three heartbeats. People seriously underestimated how fast a dancer could move.

"I mean, he's okay. Nobody died or got hurt or anything," Juli's voice called after her, but Lilias barely heard.

All right, she whispered to herself as she took the stairs two at a time. *Lord Seymere being waylaid is bad. Very bad. But I have an excuse. I'm not ashamed of where I went; I refuse to be ashamed. I'll give the captain an earful. I'll apologize. I'll lose my job. But that drunk is getting a—* With a hard shove, she flung the door leading to District Three's main office open so forcefully, its knob bounced against the wall and started swinging back towards her.

"Captain, sir, I—" But it wasn't Trevisa Mallory at the desk, that greedy, gambling, chronically sauced lordling, who only held the position as master of the Prevecost city guard because his family could think of no other way to get him out of the house.

No, it was *him*. Chaucer Seymere. The Unmaker.

Lilias wasn't sure if she bowed; maybe she curtsied. *Maybe I should just back out the door and go dig my own grave.*

"Khove, is it?"

Huh. The man seated before her wasn't as imposing in real life as he should be; all children were brought up to believe the Unmaker was a giant—whether monster or savior depended on the parent telling the story. Either way, he was the man who single-handedly had brought down a centuries-old royal house.

He had been the last de Glas king's steward. When the dragonborn had invaded those few decades ago, the lords of Albidon had betrayed the king into their hands and left him to rot in captivity. Chaucer Seymere had led that coup, lying to the king, telling him the lords of the counties would back him. They had in a way, if a knife to the back counted.

Together, steward and lords had unmade a royal dynasty, but only Seymere had gotten the epithet "Unmaker." Today, he was generally considered a national hero and sat as parliament's head most sessions. Basically, he was still a steward. Maybe the man liked life that way. *Tainted take it, I'm about to find out just what he does and doesn't like.*

"Tell me, dimilessa, why did you leave your post?"

So, right to the point. Lilias drew in a breath. The fire in her blood had dampened to sputtering sparks. Blasting Trevisa was one thing. His lazy hind end was the perfect place to unload what she'd seen tonight. He wouldn't have cared one ha'penny. But Lilias would have felt better at least giving him five minutes of having to hear about it. But even royalist's children didn't lambast the Unmaker, particularly ones who'd broken their beat. But maybe... She pulled in another breath, then let it go like a lasso.

"I apologize, my lord." She dropped into what she hoped was a decent bow. "I heard screaming in Dockside. It sounded like a child. I couldn't leave it. But my actions put citizens like yourself in danger. I'm sorry, very sorry. But please, if you would be so merciful, let me resign. Don't fire me, and please listen to what I found." Chords, what was she even saying? Firing her would be the mercy. Arresting her would be the more probable thing about to happen. Listening? Pfft.

The silence that filled the room as she finished was heavy. If her heart hadn't been pounding so loudly, she might have been able to hear the sands falling in the hourglass perched on the windowsill.

"Hmm. How about you stop bending over like a crane pecking in a pond and tell me what you found."

The *tsk* of velvet shifting against leather pulled Lilias' eyes up from the floor. The Unmaker had settled his slim form back in the bulky chair and was looking at her. Intently? Curiously? Well, he was looking and he was asking. Waiting.

Straightening her spine, Lilias slipped into a dancer's resting pose, at ease but ready to spring into motion at any sound.

Here goes nothing.

"Ships aren't unloading at the docks, my lord. The children who work there have no pay. No food." She couldn't believe she was just repeating the words the boy had said to her earlier. They weren't elegant or grand, the sort of thing that moved the masters of this world. But they were true words. Raw and honest.

"I'm aware of the situation with the Jays, dimilessa."

Somewhere in the brevity of her speech, the Unmaker had leaned forward and now his hands were interlocking their fingers into a tight, inflexible clench.

"If it's charity they need, they can go to the High Sanct. There is no law that closed the port. Ships just don't want to dock, or if they have, they don't want the crew unloading cargo. In short, they don't want contact with the city. Therefore, there is nothing *legally* I can do about this. Truly, I am sorry, but what you assume is within my power, is not."

"But—" A sharp shake of the Unmaker's head cut her off.

"I will tell you the same thing I told the little band of royalist rebels in the square. The sanctuary is for kindness." His fingers unfurled from their clench and one hand smacked down on the right side of the table. "The government is for law and order." The other hand came down on the left. "I cannot force foreign ships to do what they don't want to do, and I cannot simply legislate the sky to rain gold lions or silver cubs. But back to charity, think about it truly. If every parishioner gave the High Sanct every coin in their possession and the Elder in turn gave it all away, then what? You've only smothered the problem with metal; you have *fixed* nothing."

As if to punctuate his words further, the Unmaker suddenly reached down into a side drawer in the desk and pulled out a leather pouch, jingling with coins. Without ceremony, he dumped them onto the table. "Your district's late pay, I believe? It's short a few cubs. I'm afraid those were turned into ale by your former captain."

Former? Lilias' mind was still spinning with the Unmaker's speech, trying to find some loophole she could throw back at him.

"Yes," he went on as if reading her thoughts—and ignoring some of them. "Trevisa Mallory can drink himself into a stupor on his own time. The captain of the Falcons is your new commander."

Try as she might, Lilias couldn't contain her guffaw. "The Falcons?" she choked out. "The most expensive, gilded group of mercenary knights in Eorne? And their captain is condescending to take over the city guard? You can't be serious!" But this was the Unmaker; he was all things serious.

"The Falcons are not mercenaries, dimilessa. They are sworn to the count of Prenzlau who in turn swears fealty to the duke of Iarla, who of course, was once sworn to the king. Our monarchs always feared the personal armies of their lords, so sent those armies off to fight the wars of other royals. But the Falcons belong to Albidon and Albidon they will now serve. But don't fret, young lady." He stood and started rounding the desk, making the room and the chance of further debate, very small. "Captain Desmond Edenry is a thinking man, just what this city needs."

The Unmaker folded his arms as he drew in front of her. This close Lilias could see the full depth of his gaze. There was something there, a hurt, an understanding, a fire fueled by mercy, but smothered and held in check by years of justice and hard choices. A strange balance, a bit of truth maybe to all sides of the stories told about him.

"You see, law and charity only go so far in times of peace or of trouble. What we need now are plans, people who see and don't walk away. They think." He tapped his brow then slid the tapping down to his chin, his brow furrowed in mimic contemplation. "And then they do something. What I can do for the Jays is give this city Desmond Edenry. What he does? Well, that will be something interesting to see, indeed. Keep your job, dimilessa. I think you and the captain might just get along."

"But the watch has no jurisdiction in Dockside. How—"

But the Unmaker cut her off with a wink and another tap on his forehead. "Remember, thinking."

With that he moved past her and on towards the door. She expected him to keep going; it wasn't like these sorts of conversations ended with chitchat about local newborns, but then he paused, hand suddenly cast out to grip the door frame. His eyes didn't meet hers; his gaze had fallen far away as if he was seeing something in the past or maybe the future. Or maybe both... The sudden shift in mood caught Lilias' breath and gripped at her throat.

"Dimilessa?" the Unmaker started, his voice low but heavy with something. Foreboding? Sorrow? "I'm giving you a second chance with your job. I want you to give me something in return. Desmond Edenry isn't just a clever tactician, he's a good man, a rare man. But from my experience, such men, they bleed. They see too much; live too hard, and in the end, it takes their life too soon. Take care of him for me, eh?"

Somewhere in the speech, his gaze had finally found hers again and Lilias felt a wave of shock roll through her at the intensity and pleading in his eyes.

What in the name of sense? Her held breath came out in a cough. Woodenly, she nodded; there wasn't any other reaction to such a request, no matter how little she understood it...or intended to obey. But apparently it was enough for the Unmaker. Without another word, he was gone. Lilias stood frozen in the middle of the room listening to the fading sound of his velvet train sweeping down the hall.

What was that about? Lilias sputtered as she finally jerked life back into her limbs and turned back to the desk. After a moment's contemplation, she pounced on the coins still scattered across its surface. *What is basically anything about?* Grabbing up what was due her, she pocketed her pay and started down the hall herself. She was tired; she was hungry; whatever energy or passion had driven her the past few hours was starting to drain away. A feeling, distant but familiar, was beginning to worm its way in instead.

Her father had been a royalist. He had spent so many years trying to put one of the de Glas princes back on a throne half the kingdom declared no longer existed. She had watched him believe in something, fight for it, live for it, until finally they'd locked him away and thrown the key down some bottomless hole.

Personally, she had never been interested in who ran the country. But what she'd seen from her father had molded her in another way, carving out a heart that believed caring was like binding an impossible weight to one's shoulders. The burden of it, the fifty-to-fifty chance of never seeing your dream realized was too much to bear. So, she had closed her eyes to the world around her, clenched her fists and lived—existed. She had always known it wasn't true living, but then again, the dead feel no pain. Only the living know of hurt.

But tonight, she had felt for a brief moment what it was like to see again. Maybe even to do a little good, bring a little light. But there had been nothing easy about it.

Light creates shadows. Better to die in the dark.

As she trudged down the stairs to the main floor, head down to avoid questions and gossips, her eyes caught sight of the city through the open door, a city trapped in a struggle between life and death. *Maybe it's always about living or dying. Everything, every day—but, at least sometimes, we get to make the choice.*

PhantomRin.

THREE

It had been two days since her conversation with the Unmaker, two days Lilias had not been scheduled for a shift. So, she'd spent the time at Dockside looking for any sight of her children.

She was calling them that, she told herself, because they had *her* key. Nothing more. No attachments. No claiming or getting further involved. The reasoning worked every now and then, but mostly, she just ran, her footsteps pounding across the cobblestones and brick paveways with anxious desperation rising in every footfall. She had tried the door at the end of Rue Mahi more than once, but each time, it was locked tight. *What if they hadn't found the door, or what if the stashed supplies had been moved and the little ones were now starving and what if...how will I...and—*

The churning inside her felt like the rising waters of the sea hammering at a dike. Eventually, something would have to break. But she couldn't stop.

"Almighty," she finally puffed in a clouded breath of frustration as the sinking evening sun began to close out her final hour of freedom the second day. "What am I going to do? Why me? Why me?" She was pretty sure many people asked God that same question every day. Probably every hour. Only an all-holy being would have the patience and kindness not to eventually snarl back with the same question.

That night her shift was quiet; in the sky, the bright full moon shone down on the city like a watchful, curious eye. But as the hours tolled by, mist rolling in from the sea began to hang heavy in the air. Over Dockside, the haze seemed to pulse across the building peaks with a strange orange light. By the time four was called by the High Sanct bells, the distinct smell of too much smoke was starting to swipe through Lilias' every inhale. It wasn't chimney smoke...

She was just past Devran Square when she heard her name.

"Khove! Khove! Oh, for mercy's sake, girl, where are you?"

It was Deods. Lilias recognized the swing of the man's footsteps from the other night as he drew closer. "Here, I'm over here." Stepping under the shelter of a shuttered bookshop, she set her light on the stoop and waited.

"Ah, there you are. Chords." Without further explanation, he waved a small letter in her face with the same jerking motions his round chest was doing with its breaths.

Lilias flipped the note open with one upjerk of her thumb.

Please come to Hospice aa Aami. Urgent.
D. Edenry

Lilias took in the words once, then twice.

"What the heck?" Her face screwed into a question mark as her eyes snapped to Deods'.

But the other guard just shrugged, still breathing hard. "I don't know; you know the Falcons are taking over the watch, yeah? Well, nobody ever expected to actually see any of them. There's night watch and day watch and usually it's all run by sergeants. Trevisa was only around 'cause it was a good place to down the ale." He paused and huffed for a moment. "But the Falcon's captain came yesterday and again tonight after you left. But then he went running down to the docks. I don't know what happened. Something bad. I was about to find out when this note came from him. It was for you. So, here. I gave it to you. What's it say?"

Albidonis loved many things, but they loved stories above all else. It was their gift, the blessing given them by the Almighty at the Dawn. But on ordinary days, gossip and other people's news was as free and available a story as most folks got.

"It says to go to the hospice. I—" Lilias felt her confusion suddenly replaced with a thump of dread. Her mind raced with the names of those she knew, those close enough to warrant her name being the one they called for when sickness or hurt had sent them seeking the wisdom only the physicians of aa Aami knew. She could only think of her babka, safely hundreds of miles away and her da, also away, behind fortress walls.

"Am I going to get in trouble for this?" Lilias rattled the letter in the air.

Deods shoved his features into a flatlined pucker. "I don't know? Orders are from the captain, so I'd say you'd get into more trouble ignoring them."

He was probably right. Lilias flipped the paper over and looked at the front. No name. So, the captain didn't know her name.

"How did you know this was for me if my name isn't on it?"

"Oh." The old guard's expression flattened even further then suddenly lit up. "It was his squire who brought the note—knights have squires, you know—anyway, he said to give it to the Jay-helping girl. That's you."

Oh, joy, a nickname. Did everyone under God's sun know of her escapade, now? Either way, it meant one of two things—the new captain had been apprised of what had happened a few nights earlier and had simply labeled her because it. The letter was its own travesty to unravel. Or—he'd heard, labeled her, and it was all connected. For the first time that night, Lilias let herself truly look down at Dockside. Something...something big was burning down there.

"I don't know anything else." Deods interrupted her thoughts; the man was already starting to walk away. Everything about his posture said, "What I don't know about, I'm going to learn about. A horde of rabid monkeys won't stop me and definitely not more questions from you."

Hospice aa Aami was in District One. *It's going to take me half an hour to get there and all of it uphill.* Lilias threw another glance towards Dockside. Whatever was happening down there, she was pretty sure the real answer would only cough itself up if she followed orders. So, with one hand, she stuffed the note into her vest pocket and with the other, she yanked up her light. Then with both legs, one moving after the other, she started towards District One.

Lilias had never been inside Hospice aa Aami, just glimpsed the odd feat of architecture—white limestone and glass all molded into a sprawling triangle—many times. The place was centuries old, but its gleaming walls still glittered in the pre-dawn light as Lilias finally found herself just outside its main courtyard.

"Plague business or other?"

Lilias jumped at the sudden sound of the voice; her whole body skittered at least a pace to the left. In the dim light, she hadn't noticed the gates were completely shut and a solitary guard stood just behind the skull-shaped lock. As her eyes focused on the shadowy figure, she had to shove back a laugh. He was definitely not aware of it, but the man's every feature was in the process of redefining boredom.

"What?"

"Plague business or other?" the voice repeated.

"I'm here at the orders of Captain Edenry."

"Never heard of him. Plague business or other?" *Okay, no longer amusing.*

Lilias might have spent the rest of her sunrises trying to explain to Guard Can't Think Past Two Options when a young voice rang out through the frosty air.

"Figs and thistles, she's with me. Let her in, why don't you, already!"

Lilias couldn't see the speaker. But she was pretty sure whoever he was, he wasn't Captain Edenry. The voice was a boy's voice, one who hadn't quite finished informing himself he was going to be a man someday.

Lilias didn't wait for Guard Two Options to open the gate more than a crack before she squeezed through.

"Ah, there you are." The voice had started again, its owner becoming clearer as Lilias moved further into the courtyard. "I would say I'd been waiting, but I just got here myself."

Closer up confirmed Lilias' suspicions. The youth, with his mess of curls and round, lavender eyes, couldn't have been past fifteen, dressed in clothing that was simple, but well-made, the sort of ensemble knights gave their squires.

It was his squire that brought the note—

Aha.

"Come along." The lad waved. His movement might have been an attempt at playing the leader, but it completely lacked any authority. Not with that squeaky voice.

Lilias found herself with the urge to smile again.

"Do you know what's going on in Dockside?" she asked as they stepped through a narrow door carved into the limestone.

"Yes, yes, of course, I do. Wait, dimilessa, you're going the wrong way!"

Lilias felt a hand wrap around the silk of her sleeve and tug her with one fierce pull.

"That way is the plague ward." A shudder jiggled the boy's shoulders. "Down there is teeming with nasty. We're going this way." He pointed at another corridor. "Chords, we don't need you going the wrong way. I mean, if you've had the ragers as a wee one you'd be okay, they say? Can't get shadowpox then. Have you had the ragers, dimi?"

This boy would make conversations with fence posts. "Yes, I have actually. The docks?" Lilias found herself lengthening her strides to keep up—and raising her voice to redirect the rambling downspin of the conversation.

"Oh, yes." The young squire whirled mid step and flashed a toothy grin. Lilias had almost missed her people's obsession with hearing and telling anything that resembled interesting during her years away. *Almost.*

"So. Last night, some of the Jays raided an Athlander ship. Got away with quite a bit of goods before they were run off. Maybe it would have all been all right, crew tried to keep it quiet, but word got back to their shipmaster and he bloody popped." The boy was talking and walking so fast now, Lilias was beginning to think his family should have apprenticed him to an auctioneer instead of a knight. "Tonight, he ordered his men off the ship and then torched the whole thing."

Lilias stopped so hard her boots snagged in the thick carpet. "So, he would rather his men be right here in the city where there *is* sickness, than on a ship where it *might* have been?"

"Dimilessa, the master of that ship is current consort to the Black Widow Queen herself. Brains are lacking in all departments where he's concerned."

The Black Widow Queen? Lilias' mind let out a whistle. No wonder the captain of the city guard's presence had been required. Queen Rhysana of Atherland was a powerful monarch, world-renowned beauty—and husband killer. She wanted twins and pity spare the man who didn't give them to her. But whatever man was her current consort *was* a king, pitiable or not.

"Well." That was about all there was to say to that.

"Eh, Captain settled things down, but then the sparks shooting off the ship caught onto some barrels of whiskey. Quite the bang. Captain got burned." The lad stopped walking midsentence, his brow puckering into a worried look. "I don't think it was too bad, though. They said it wasn't."

Oh, chords, I didn't get called here to play nursemaid to a grown man, did I? Lilias knew she was one of the city's newest guards, but still, that didn't mean they could make her a servant. Could they?

"It was the girl who looked worse," the boy went on. "She kept asking for you. So, Captain said we had to find you. He's—"

"Girl, what girl?" If Lilias had been slapped with a lash made of al'am eels, she couldn't have felt a greater jolt than ran through her at the word "girl."

"Jay girl from down at the docks; she got hit by the firestorm pretty bad. Captain got her out. That's how he got hurt. He brought her here. Otherwise, I'm pretty sure he wouldn't have bothered for himse—"

But Lilias was already starting to run, the anxiety that had driven her for the past few days roaring to life with full fury.

"Dimi!"

Don't let my girl be dead. I don't even know her name, but blessed Almighty, let her be okay.

With her guide now paces behind her, Lilias really wasn't sure where she was going. Straight ahead seemed the most logical. The corridor was a long one, lined on one side by floor to ceiling stained glass windows and closed doors every few feet on the other. There. Leaning beside the final door just before the corridor split three ways, was a man.

His clothes were not that of the city guard. Lilias recognized the black leathers and sky-blue shirt. Falcon colors. As she drew closer, she could see the man was on the older end of young with features too round to be rugged but too big-boned to be boyish. In one hand, he was tossing an apple up and down and with the other, he rapped some tune on the wall with his fingers. He looked and seemed pleasant enough.

Pleasant is good, but I thought a captain would be older?

"Are you Captain Edenry?" she asked, skidding to a stop and dropping a bow. Who cared how old he was—the girl, the Jays, that's what mattered.

"Huh?" The Falcon caught his apple then pushed himself off the wall with a single movement. Up close, he was taller than he'd seemed. "Me? Eh, no." His voice was soft-spoken; he didn't sound like he could or ever had harmed more than a fly. But the muscles that made his vest creak as he folded his arms said otherwise. He shook his head then jerked it in the direction of the door. "He is. Hey, Des!"

Okay, deep breath, this is it.

There was silence for half a heartbeat, then a face peered around the door accompanied by a bare shoulder. There was a look in her direction, then a yelp. The owner of the face yanked whatever fabric was in his hand up over his naked chest, and the door swung back shut with a slam.

No.

Lilias felt her mind join the yelp, but hers was more like a scream.

No.

PhantomRin.

FOUR

Chords in flats and sharps, no! She knew him. That face, with its flaring slash of jaw and harsh cheekbones, all framed by auburn hair. She would never forget that face—or its expression as she had cursed his heartbeat to the Pale Mercy. Poor man.

Anybody but him!

It had been two years ago, at the peak of the White Poppy War. Lilias had still been with the Troupe Beli back then. They'd stopped in the Masque for a four-night show. Everything had gone all right—or as all right as dancing in the Masque could go. Men there didn't understand true art. All they wanted to see was something the Troupe Beli did *not* do. So, the audience had been mostly women and children. Not bad. But the attitude of the male population had quickly gotten under Lilias' skin—probably as much as the men felt irked about not getting to see what was underneath her costume.

Maybe the visit would have become as unmemorable as a grey sky, but on the last night in the city, the master had sent her to running—stage makeup, costume and all—to the moneylenders. Their passage had been paid with the wrong currency; they ran the risk of losing their place on the ship or some such stuff and aggravation.

Anyway, Lilias had gone. To the wrong address, apparently. Because all she got was a lone, young man, dressed in Albidoni fashion, answering her knock with the most bewildered look on his face. And that's when it had happened—

He'd thought she was a courtesan. With a stammer, he had asked her to leave. With that much makeup on and dressed like something from fairytale land, she couldn't say she had ever blamed him. But it was the city, the lustful mood. It all came out. Of her mouth.

May the Pale Mercy spit on you! she'd shouted. It was the darkest curse she knew, the darkest one anyone this side of the Feathered Wastes knew. His poor, innocent face had gone from bewildered to panicked, a deep, scarlet shade shooting across his rugged features. Without another word, she'd stormed off into the evening light.

She had always regretted her words, her reaction—not the anger that had driven them—but, poor man. He'd just been in the wrong place at the wrong time. Well, *she* had been in the wrong place. Either way. Lilias never could recall how they'd straightened out the travel situation. She had gotten home somehow. All the way to right now...

"That the way they're wearing shirts now, Des? All wadded up?" The apple-tossing Falcon's chuckle snapped her mind back into the present. The awful present.

He must hate me; surely, he hates me.

There was a primal grumble from behind the door, some rustling of fabric, the sound of a belt latching, and then, Lilias could hear it, a hand pulling the knob back. Instinctively, she slammed her eyelids shut. It was simple, she told herself. *When I open them maybe Captain Edenry will have a different face. Maybe he was changing his face as well as his clothes.*

One heartbeat, two, three.

"Hey, you can look." There was a shake on her shoulder. "It's safe. He's civilized now."

"Huh?" Her eyes flew open. Both men must have thought she'd been completely scandalized or maybe was just an utter dumb-dumb. As her sight bloomed back into focus, her eyes locked with those of the man now standing directly in front of her—this Desmond Edenry, this man who was supposed to save a city, this man she was supposed to look out for...the very one she'd cursed to the whims of death herself.

Oh, I'm a dumb-dumb in so *many ways.*

By the looks of it, Desmond was younger than the Falcon she'd first met, but his gaze—Lilias expected to see plenty in it: recognition, disgust, anger, but instead, she felt her breath draw in and then, everything seemed to suspend. For one slow thump of a heartbeat, it was as if all of her—sight, soul, and being—was now washed away into something. Something other, something ancient, sweeping through her, seeing, knowing, then just as quickly, just as gently, letting go.

What in the name of sense? Lilias gave her imagination a smack and puffed out her breath. The man was just looking at her. Nothing weird, eldritch or magical. Her babka had told her too many stories of wishwalkers. But why the heck was she thinking of them now?

Maybe, in any other circumstance, the mystery of that gaze would have lingered to niggle on in the back of her mind. But there was too much already inside her head. Besides, if it was real, it meant beyond a doubt he'd recognized her. There would be no hiding, lying or trying to feign innocence.

And suddenly, desperately, she wanted him not to know her. Whatever she'd imagined or expected in his look, one thing she knew wasn't make believe. There was kindness in his pale, grey eyes, true and genuine. It was like his naive innocence she'd witnessed in the Masque, but this was honed and focused, sharp and ready. And it just might save...so many. The Unmaker may have been a crown-stealer, but he certainly wasn't a liar.

"Thank you for coming, dimilessa. I apologize for the—" The captain's voice cut through her thoughts accompanied by a hard little cough. "The strangeness of the circumstances."

Then, he bowed. It started out formally enough, but ended in a sloppy hurry, like he'd forgotten certain parts of his body had been singed and he was happy to just get it over with.

Maybe...maybe, he doesn't know me?

"Captain, sir!" The sound was as unmusical as an out of tune harp.

His squire. Lilias had forgotten her little guide. But the boy came running up at that moment, huffing and panting, and would have collided head to stomach with his master had the other Falcon not caught him by the collar.

"Look here, Alston Roland," the man started. "Can you do anything right? You were supposed to be tending the young lady, but no, you're dragging behind and—"

"I tried, lieutenant, sir, *she—* "The boy, apparently from House Roland, twisted in his superior's grasp and gave Lilias a judging look. "Ran off on me. By my honor!"

Lilias flicked her eyes over to the captain to gauge his reaction. To her surprise, Desmond laughed. It wasn't loud, in fact, she doubted there was much effort behind it at all. But it was easy-going all the same.

Maybe he's the true laid back one.

"Antony, take young Roland back to the Roost."

"Me?" The apple-tossing Falcon looked like he'd just been asked to dance with wild bears. "Why do I have to deal with him?"

At this, Desmond's mouth widened and tightened all at once. "Because, right now, I'm feeling like you two deserve each other." Everything in his smile and look said that his displayed nakedness was not about to be forgiven just yet.

Okay, maybe not laid back.

It was with more chattering, collar hauling and general rowdiness than was probably necessary, but the squire and Falcon lieutenant finally disappeared around the corner.

"This way, if you would." Desmond stuck out a hand indicating a small, narrow passage Lilias hadn't noticed before.

Mutely, she obeyed, falling into step not quite beside him, but close enough to be heard. If she could summon the courage.

"Have we met before?" The words were out of her mouth before she could stop them. *Ack!* Her common sense screamed. *Why? I thought you hoped he didn't know? Why? Because,* her nerves snarled back, *better to have it over and done. Oh, it's done now,* said common sense, slinking inward with a wounded *I told you so. Everything is done.*

"Hmm? Met? No." Desmond turned slightly as he replied.

Well, then.

Sunny skies, fluffy rabbits and all the good things in the world. Moving on! As if her legs had read her mind, Lilias' pace quickened until she found herself walking stride to stride with the captain.

"Your squire said something about a Jay girl? What happened? Is she all right?" All the nervous energy that had been swimming inside her for the past few days had risen back up now, shoving her brief relief aside and refocusing her mind.

"Yes, I'm to understand you were of some assistance to a group of Jays a few nights back? Apparently, you made an impression on one of them," he answered. "There was an incident a few hours ago in Dockside. We were able to get a lass out before it got too bad. I hoped she would lead us to some sort of adult down there who's responsible for this lot, but she just kept asking for you. So, here you are."

Lilias' mind made quick work of two things. First, the squire had said Desmond alone had pulled the young Jay away from the fire. He however had said, "we." Self-deprecating much? Or was Alston over-dramatic? Either seemed possible. Second, was his last line. It could mean a general phrase of "and that's the sum of everything." Or—

Oh, no. With a silent push of a handle, the captain was opening the door he'd stopped in front of. That meant...that meant the little girl was on the other side. Suddenly, Lilias wasn't ready for that. Stepping through meant actually committing, staying, seeing it through. She was *supposed* to be a dancer, traveling the world, never making roots, never staying long enough to build bonds. *Why am I here!* Everything that had conflicted her for so long bubbled to the surface.

"I don't... I—" She felt her body start to turn.

"Wait!"

A hand caught her sleeve. The captain's voice was quiet, hushed like a prayer, but his hold was strong, like a plea too desperate for words. She threw a glare up at him but didn't pull away.

"I didn't send for you to play nurse if such a thing puts you off. If you're squeamish, that is. If that's what's worrying you. I just thought—" He paused, eyes slipping from hers till they found some distant spot. "I just thought maybe the girl meant something to you. Forgive me, I misunderstood." His voice grew hard at the last sentence and when he finished, he dropped his hand away and bent into another bow. This one however lasted even less time than the first. "Chords," he swore, catching at his side.

Lilias thew out her hand. "Stop, just stop bobbing at me like a marionette. I'm not noble, royal or important." She wasn't sure what she intended to do with her outstretched hand, if she meant to push him away, or maybe push him back up—a generally stupid idea for one to do to a stranger who was both injured and a superior—she didn't know what her hand was going to do. Treacherous thing that it was, it caught the door handle instead.

Silent but swift, the door swung open. The room that came into view was a small one, its only furniture a little trundle bed nestled against the far wall with a high, narrow table just behind it. The room's only occupant lay curled on the bed wrapped up in sheets and what looked like someone's cloak. Black with a pale blue silk lining. Falcon colors.

Lilias' legs joined her hand in rebellion and started pushing her into the room.

"For mercy's sake, don't wake her."

The sound of Desmond's voice sent a jolt through her spine, pulling her whole body and senses into the realization that she really was doing this. "Huh?"

"Look, I don't know anything about children, but I know if they're sleeping, you never, ever wake them."

There was such a look of dead earnestness in the man's face, Lilias couldn't help but laugh—silently, but her sides quivered all the same.

"There might be some scarring but all the smoke the lass took in was the main worry," he continued softly, coming up beside her and either not seeing or choosing to ignore her amusement. "But it could have been worse."

"Pfft, says a man who's seen people's insides draped over their outsides."

"I've seen worse." The repeated words had that same frozen tone he'd used earlier.

Touchy, touchy.

"Dimi?" a little voice murmured from the bed. "Did you come see me? Is it a dream?"

Lilias glanced over at Desmond, but the man made no show of moving. *All right, then.* "Shh, no, I'm right here," she said easing herself down onto the trundle's narrow edge, the silk of her uniform making its own shushing sound as it brushed against the bedding. Arms latched around her neck an instant later.

"I was so scared." The Jay's words came out in a rush. "It was so bright and so hot. It hurt. It still hurts."

"Shh, it's okay now. You should be sleeping. You need sleep. Everything is all right. Shh."

Gently, Lilias stroked her hand against the girl's hair. *Maybe this is a little like what a mother feels when she first holds her newborn.* The rest of the girl looked clean, but her hair was still a twist of tangled braids.

Lilias scrunched her nose. "You need something done with this hair."

"If you want her to smell like a girl, I'd suggest something of yours." Desmond had come a few steps closer. With his ramrod straight posture and hands clasped behind his back, he looked like a bodyguard. *He is, stupid. A well paid, international one who is now your boss.* "Anything I have will turn heads thinking she's joined the army."

"Hmm." Lilias sniffed consideringly. "Some ladies like pine tar, I'll have you know."

"Are you all right, sir?" The little girl had lifted her head from Lilias, and was looking towards Desmond.

"Oh, he's fine. He's seen worse." Lilias thew Desmond a look that said, *keep this funny; keep it light.*

"Hey! She was asking if I *felt* worse. There's a difference."

Against Lilias' shoulder, the Jay giggled, then said, "What's your name, dimi? I know his."

"Hmm? Oh, my name?" In Albidon, honorifics were a strange thing. What you did, what you said depended on the county you came from. But in each region, one thing was a certainty, to give your birth name upon meeting was a sign of deep commitment, a pledge that whatever was between two people was forever.

"Lilias, my name is Lilias. Yours?"

"Ani. It's Ani."

Probably short for something. Maybe named for the father.

"Well, that seems easy enough to remember. Now." Lilias stood, shoving any feelings or thoughts of what she had just done down as deep as they would go. "We should see about getting you something nice—"

Oh, chords. Chords. She shouldn't have looked down. The captain had actually gotten one thing right earlier. She *was* squeamish, can't-stand-a-rare-steak squeamish. And right there, right by her boots was the only other thing in the room, a wastebin. It wasn't full but there were enough old, bloody rags in it. Just enough to—

"Excuse me." She tried for grace, but all that came out was a gag as she shoved past Desmond and was out of the room faster than she'd ever moved in her life.

"And that, my lady and eavesdropping birdies, is our show for today. Thank you for watching." The bizarre words were followed by the fading sounds of footsteps, the click of a shutting door and a grunt of pain.

Why must he blooming bow to everything? But Lilias didn't have time to feel anything more about the captain's cover up of her hasty exit. A door, she needed outside, now.

There. Inset into one of the stained-glass windows was a vertical latch. Grabbing it, she turned and prayed that it wasn't decorative. At the force of her hand, the half window, half door flew open. Cold, dawn air rushed into her lungs. Doubling over, she clutched her knees and heaved.

But it was a futile effort. As nothing came out, memory threw itself back in. It was an old habit, forgetting to eat, one she'd picked up in her youth as training would lose her for hours on end in the music and the movements.

"When's the last time you ate?"

Drawing a hand over her dry mouth, Lilias stumbled to get upright. Desmond was standing over her; he must have followed her out. She could make out the outline his shadow cast against the white arch beside her. At her swaying movements, his hand went to her back, but then didn't release. He expected an answer. She could see the determination in his eyes as her head turned towards his.

"I, uh, I guess I forgot."

Incredulity widened his eyes. "How does one *forget* to eat?"

"I don't know? You just do? Haven't you?" Her legs were still shaking and she suddenly felt too tired to argue. She cast him a look up and down. He was probably just at six feet tall, average build, but strong. But there were shadows in the hollows underneath his sharp cheekbones that told the story of a man who had not spent much time in his life banqueting.

"I was a prisoner of war once, dimilessa, and I assure you I tallied every meal I was missing."

"I'm sorry." The words came out in a mumble, but she meant it. Genuinely, she did. A guilty feeling niggled in the back of her mind. *I wonder if he considered that experience worse than getting cursed by an over-painted tantrum thrower?*

Desmond's only answer however was to suddenly start patting across the suede front of his jerkin as if looking for something.

"Ah." Without further formality, he withdrew a slim flask. Its silver casing shimmered in the dawn light as he held it out to her.

She shook her head. "Thank you, I don't drink."

He didn't pull the flask away. "Neither do I."

Well, then.

Lilias was never sure afterwards which of them made the first move to sit on the little granite bench that rested under an arbor of wilting autumn roses.

The stone was cold, but its support felt like a miraculous hug. Lilias stretched out her legs, letting the toe tips of her boots click together. "Ah, you never forget how glorious sitting is until you've done hours of walking." *Or, how hungry you are until suddenly you've tried to eject the contents of your stomach to no avail.* She tipped the flask back. The wild tang of apples and spices shot through her senses and slid down her throat. Leers cider. Fresh and sublime.

"Thank you, for covering my exit," she said, mouth tanging with cinnamon. "I hope she didn't notice?"

"No, just laughed. Apparently, you have a funny face."

Lilias ignored that. "So, birdies?"

"What about them?" Desmond was propping an elbow onto the bench's side arm.

"Birdies," Lilias repeated. "You said it to the girl. It's a funny word for grownups to say. Do you have little siblings, then?" She took another long swig. Maybe too much sugar was making her too bold...

"I don't have siblings or children, but—" He paused, a screwed expression creasing his face. "I have an Artair. That counts for all things juvenile."

Lilias had heard of Artair d'Argon, count of Prenzlau and chosen successor to the Unmaker. To the people, he had another title as well.

"The Golden Godsent is your friend?"

At that Desmond fairly bristled. "Chords, don't call him that. It gives him grand ideas."

Or other people ideas. There were two stories about the Golden Godsent. Some said they were legends, others called them prophecies, but both were about a man of pure sunlight who came to bathe the world in goodness. One story said he did and all was well for centuries to come. The other told of his light drowned out by shadows and rivers of blood. Only ashes left to remain. Apparently, Artair believed one and Desmond feared the other...

"What about the Jays?" It probably wasn't Lilias' business what the captain planned to do for the Dockside tykes. The man probably didn't know himself yet. But anything to change the subject.

"Ah yes, that matter." Desmond straightened and clamped his hands on his knees, a sudden light coming into his eyes. "Well, they're message runners and parcel carriers already, yes? So, they can do that for the entire city. There's many who don't want to go out now or can't if there's sickness inside the house." He shrugged. "So, the Jays can do it. No work at the docks doesn't mean there isn't work. Put it in the broadsheets, word of mouth. It will spread."

Lilias blinked. *Definitely too much sugar.* "That fast?" She snapped her fingers together as her eyes locked on his. "You've thought up a solution already? How fast does your mind work, anyway?" She tipped the flask again if only to stop more words from coming out of her mouth.

But Desmond just laughed. "When a volley of arrows is flying at you, pretty tainted fast you'd better hope."

"True." Lilias handed the flask back to him. The weight of it was considerably lighter, but if the captain noticed it didn't show on his face. "I suppose that's fun to imagine—the idea for the children, not the arrows—" she clarified. "Food, packages, tonics to deliver, love letters." She sighed and stretched her legs longer. "Maybe even the latest aria for an opera singer."

A choking noise came from Desmond.

"What, you don't like opera? I know it's new, but it's so fascinating."

"If I want to hear sounds like that," he said, "I'll go to the mountains and watch two wildcats fight over territory."

Lilias might have laughed, belly hard and side-splitting, totally and forever ruining whatever opinion this man and his defunct memory had of her. But a voice from the door she'd exited just minutes ago, startled her sober.

"Excuse me," the young woman said, "the matron was wanting to know whose name should be put on the tab for the burn victim brought in earlier. I was told to ask either of you."

Lilias stood. But so did Desmond, his larger form blocking her line of sight and voice.

"Mine," he said. "Desmond Edenry."

"I can pay. I want to help." Lilias pinched his sleeve and when that got her nothing, she poked his ribs, her finger connecting with too much padding—bandages. He grunted. She jumped back. From here, she could see that the woman had already retreated into the hospice again. *Chords.*

"If you want to do something charitable, take your money and put food in your stomach. I'm sure it would consider anything a kindness." Desmond rounded back facing her again. Lilias folded her arms, but at the sight of his expression, the fight drained from her. He looked so weary, the kind that doesn't start but is always just there, only now and then rising enough to the surface to be seen. *It's been a long night for him.*

"Fine, fine." Throwing her hands up palms out in surrender. "There's a *blin* cart in Rue de Clare; I'll bring back something for our little friend. And a brush and some things from my flat." Lilias scrunched her face, wondering if she had any clothes that could be workable.

"Hmm, sounds like a handful; Alston can help you. Where—" Desmond's head spun in an arc. "Where is that rascal? Oh." He puffed his breath. "Never mind, I'll do it myself." He started forward but then paused, rocking slightly on his toes as if time had clamped him into place. "That is, if you don't object?"

Lilias shook her head and shrugged, her eyes widening a little. "It's far, but your legs, your choice. Uh, sir." Suddenly, she was struck with how utterly informally she'd been speaking to him. But he waved her off, already heading for the door.

"You're off duty, consider yourself off duty."

They walked together in silence through the hospice grounds and on past the gate. The sky had been trading darkness for light for some time, but it seemed to be moving slowly this morning. The paler colors came in slashes, like time was drumming its fingers, waiting for something. Along the streets, mist still hung thick in the air. "I know poppypaste dulls the appetite," Lilias said, finally breaking the quiet as they neared Preve Bridge. "But I think I can find something that will tempt her."

"How did you know they'd given her that?"

She laughed. "I could smell it. I used to be a dancer. We went through poppypaste by the jar almost every night."

"Ah," was Desmond's only response. But Lilias cast a little glance sideways at him. He really must not remember her. *Just fine with me. This might not be so bad after all.* Lilias had no intentions of staying in the city guard. As soon as she could find a position, she would return to a dance company. But until then—a man kind and clever wasn't a bad superior. And so easy to fluster. *If I hadn't made you suffer so much before, I'd have fun with that, Captain Edenry.*

In the mist, Preve Bridge, with its pale color and high arched center, was almost impossible to see. Only the sound of gravel changing to smooth stone under their booted feet let her know they were now making the crossing. But as they rose higher, rays of light began to break away the fog.

"Look!" Lilias felt her breath catch in her throat. *It's so beautiful.* It was hard to tell where on the bridge they were; mist still danced around their feet. But the sky had opened, vast and wide. Peach and scarlet splashed against warming blue, kissing little clouds till they joined in the blush. Against the wash of colors, morning birds danced and sang. "It's so beautiful," she gasped again. "I've never seen anything like it."

"Hmm. Fine thing, yes."

"I haven't thanked you for saving Ani last night," Lilias said after a moment of silence. She wasn't moving, not from this sight.

"It was hard not to see."

"A lot of people wouldn't have bothered looking."

"Eh, why worry about them." Desmond had turned away from the sunrise and was leaning his back against the bridge's stone parapet, his face toward Lilias. "There's a difference, dimilessa, between looking and seeing. Everybody looks at things, but seeing is another matter entirely. Takes a little brains—" He tapped his temple. "And maybe a little heart. They exist inside us. Why not use them? No point in going to the grave with unused internal organs." He smiled at her. It wasn't a flashy, brilliant smile. In fact, Lilias wasn't sure his lips had parted at all. Just one corner of his mouth turned up.

"But how do you do it?" The question came out, hard and fast, her eyes jerking from his and fixing on the bleeding eastern sky. Her hands ground into the stone under her fingertips. It wasn't a question meant for hearing; it wasn't one meant for answering. It was just *her* question. It was one thing to know you *should* do a thing. It was one thing to be told you *should* live. But how? It felt like being asked to put out hell with a thimble. Painful, impossible.

"Oh. Well." Desmond's words came slowly this time, deliberately even, as if he was thinking and sorting things out both inside his head and out loud all at once. "It's like dawn, I suppose. The night is black as pitch, but little by little the light comes. Step by step. That's what living is. A little thing here and a little thing there, and before you know it, you've got a sunrise. You can't save the world. No one was ever asked to. That was the Almighty's job, and look how many people rejected that." He gave a grim little snort. "But he still came. What would happen to the world if the sun knew it would storm that day, so it just never rose at all? What would the world be like, then?"

"But the pain; it hurts to see."

"Hmm, I suppose you're right." Unconsciously, Desmond's hand went to his burned side. "But not as much as you'd think. I heard—oh, where is it? I wrote it down." His hand slid up and started patting his jerkin again. *Does he carry his whole world in his clothing? I thought that was something babkas did?*

"Sir!" That voice...

Lilias groaned.

Desmond laughed. "You too, eh? I keep thinking he'll grow out of it, or grow into it. Or just grow."

Out of the fading mist, like a harbinger of interruptions, rolled a carriage. Scrambling down from beside the coachman with all the energy of a honeybee was young Alston and his squeaky voice.

"Sir! My lord wants you! He's inside. He says it's urgent."

"Chords," Lilias heard Desmond sputter, hand still searching his jerkin. "Just because he's now awake doesn't mean I don't want to go to bed." Raising his voice, he said, "Alston, come here."

The boy obeyed with something involving three skips and a running leap.

"Go with the young lady and see to it you're a help, and for heaven's sake, don't burn her ears off with everything you think you know, all right?"

Desmond had the expression of someone handing a glass punch bowl to an Ipin kangaroo.

"We'll be fine. Go on." To prove her point, Lilias pulled Alston to her side and gave Desmond her best version of an assuring smile. She almost bowed, but caught herself just as her head started to dip. He'd just feel the need to return it.

"Yes, sir!" Alston saluted his master, hand open-palmed against heart.

"Ah, here, dimilessa. Maybe this will answer your question." In his hand, Desmond had an assortment of small, colored papers. One he pinched between his thumb and forefinger and extended to her.

"Giving something away can't hurt so much if it was never yours to start with." With that he smiled, pressed the slip of paper into her hand and before she could answer, had disappeared inside the carriage.

Lilias stood watching the vehicle as it rolled past. A crest with a grey and white falcon rising through the darkness was emblazoned on the door. Two male voices came from inside; one sounded amused, the other *not.*

"Do you know his lordship, Count Artair? That was him in there."

"No." Lilias pulled her eyes away from the disappearing carriage and steered her charge forward. *But I imagine I just might soon enough if things keep up this craziness.*

Alston moved forward, well, everything but his head. Craning it around, he looked at what was in Lilias' hand. "What's that, dimi?"

She'd almost forgotten the note. It was torn from something larger. A journal perhaps? The paper felt like the sort printers sewed blank between leather covers. Her eyes took in the words. The penmanship was undoubtedly the captain's. It was the embodiment of him. Precise, not too forward, not too slanted to the back. Just up and down letters, small but readable, with just a bit of flare around each new word.

"Nothing," she said, jerking her head up, her eyes suddenly burning hot with tears that threatened to spill out. "Come along, we're going to find breakfast."

At that Alston sprang ahead of her. Pity the man, beast, or cart that got in his way.

The words. Lilias cast a glance at them again. *Giving something away can't hurt so much if it was never yours to start with*, he'd said. She crushed the paper in her hand and held it to her heart as she walked. Dawn light fluttered in the corner of her eye, and a sprawling city filled the rest of her vision. She wasn't sure, but maybe her steps felt lighter. Maybe it was possible. To see, to live, to feel and not be crushed. To put out hell, as it were, even with a thimble.

After all—she looked down at the words again—

Love and life are merely gifts and they're meant to be given away.

Maybe it was true. *I suppose I'll find out.*

EPILOGUE

Oh, he remembered. Desmond Edenry wasn't a liar, but a knight knew how to hide his true face when he wanted to. And hers was one he could never forget.

And now he knew her name.

Lilias.

With a groan and a sigh that might have come out as a scream if he'd had the energy, Desmond dumped himself onto the carriage seat and closed his eyes. He was exhausted in places he hadn't before known existed as part of his makeup.

Chords, what a night. First the Athlander king, then the fire. Then her. The one and only her. It had been two years, but every day since then he'd thought of her, that spitfire with chestnut hair and eyes that danced like they'd been lit with the very essence of life itself. Oh, she'd embarrassed him. If floors could swallow men, he would have gladly drowned in wood and marble that night. But there had been something about her—

He was a soldier who'd seen death, dealt death and felt it dog his own heartbeat for so long, that he'd forgotten life was real. But, that night, he'd seen it again. Raw, rare, fiery life. It had sent a change through him, breathed hope into his shattered soul.

Some days, he felt he would go mad if he didn't see that wildcard of a woman somehow, somewhere again to thank her. And then, there she was, out of the blue. Staring at him, round eyed and gaping.

His shoulders shuddered in a cringe at the memory of the way he'd opened and then slammed the door and another groan slipped out of his lips. *Antony St. Clair, I swear I'm going to throttle you. But at least*, he thought with relief, *Tony doesn't know who she is or—Chords. Chords.* Tony might have been in the dark, but Artair: blessed, golden, blabber-mouthed Artair did know. He'd been there that night, standing just behind Desmond as he'd made the world's greatest fool of himself. And now, he was inches away again with a full view of what and who Desmond had been talking to. He could feel the man positively vibrating with recognition from where he sat opposite.

With one swift movement, Desmond swung his knees up and kicked. Artair was well past six feet tall and made of mouth and legs, but mostly legs. It didn't take more than the slightest shift to connect with the man's shins.

Anyone else would have yelled and threatened things involving the underworld. But not Artair.

"That was that woman." The voice that broke the silence had held at least five seconds longer than Desmond had expected.

He pried one eye open and gave his friend a withering look. "My, my, what observing eyes you have, old man."

Really, Artair was only fifteen months his senior; they had been inseparable for well over two decades. One a count, the other a captain. Artair existed to make the world a better place—or make a mess of it. Most of the time, like a happy puppy, he didn't know the difference. Desmond's job was to clean up those messes...it was just hard when the meddling was stirring his own life.

"Was it really her?"

Desmond scowled, pulling both eyes open and his body into a more upright position. "Yes, she doesn't remember me. I don't want to talk about it. What did *you* want to talk about? Alston said it was urgent?"

Artair was determined, but also easy to sidetrack. He opened his mouth, more questions desperately wanting to come out. But instead, he stripped off his gloves and started reaching for the leather-bound case beside him.

"Oh, yes, Parliament confirmed your position over the city guard last night. I need you to sign this." The man shuffled through at least a dozen papers before finally pulling out one sheet and waving it, seal side down, under Desmond's nose.

Desmond took it but a second later flicked his eyes back across the carriage. "This isn't mine." He didn't relinquish the document. "This is an order reinstating Nathair Mallory as general of the Iarlian regulars."

"Hmm? Oh." Artair didn't meet his gaze. "He was good at it. Why search for someone else. Better the devil you know, right?"

"A devil is still a devil! He said he was going to kill you!"

Artair growled and yanked the parchment away. "He was drunk."

"He's still drunk. Just not on liquor. Ari—" Desmond raked a hand through his hair. Artair was all the things people imagined, golden hearted and generous to a fault. And trusting. Far too trusting. Nathair Mallory had wanted the position as the

Unmaker's someday-successor. But Artair had won it instead, fair and honest.

The Tourney of Faces had been almost a decade ago, but Nathair had never forgiven his defeat at Artair's hands. He'd resigned his position as general and disappeared to his lands in the Bally—but not before swearing to bring Artair down to the grave. Artair had ignored the threat. What drunken men said in the dark they regretted in the day, he'd chirped with a smile. But Desmond knew Nathair was drunk on something else, something green and perennial—greed. And that didn't die with the dawn.

"Forget Nathair," Artair cut in. His tone, it was rare Desmond heard it directed at him, but sometimes they were count and captain, lord and underling. And Desmond had no choice but to obey.

"Here." Without further words or presentation, Artair handed Desmond another document and tapped the bottom.

This certifies Sir Desmond Edenry of Claredon as captain of the city guard of Prevecost in the duchy of Iarla, kingdom of Albidon, on this day, the fourth of the month Syl, year of Jesucrist 1021.

"Is this really what you want, Des?" Artair's voice broke over the sound of quill against parchment.

Desmond snorted. The quill in his hand took a hard spin between his fingers. "Does it matter? These are orders. Not a request."

“Someday, I promise, you’ll get to make your own choice. What you want. Whatever your dream is. I swear.”

Desmond’s eyes jerked up, locking on the opposite wall. Suddenly, there was a lump in his throat. Artair’s words were a kindness. Little more. His friend knew what he was, what he really was. What he could see in the daytime, and where his dreams took him every night. Wishwalkers, those who walked the Dream realm didn’t have dreams of their own, about themselves. To see was their blessing, to see was their curse.

Desmond had never cared. A soldier’s life made things easy. Go where you’re told. Do what you’re ordered to. Don’t dream.

But today, the thought stung. Why? Because of her...? Why did she make him want...more...

“She really didn’t know who you were? That’s not possible. Come on, Des.” Artair, ever rabbit trailing, had changed subjects again.

“I don’t know.” Desmond tossed the paper onto the seat across from him, flipping the quill with it. “Maybe she did. She asked if we’d met before.”

“And what did you say?”

“Pfft, I said no. That was certainly no true meeting in any decent person’s book.”

“So?”

Desmond knew what that question meant. *Do you feel the same about her now as you’ve felt for the past two years? Is she the same? Oh, and when should we book the High Sanct for your wedding?*

He didn’t answer. He didn’t have an answer. Crossing one leg over the other and twisting his body so that his shoulder was to

Artair, he propped his elbow onto the carriage windowsill and dropped his chin down into his palm. Artair knew after over two decades of friendship what that meant.

There was duty. Captaining a guard in a city fighting an enemy unlike anything he'd ever battled before. There was prophecy. Which story about the Golden Godsent was true? Did he sheathe his sword and bask in the sunlight, or did he watch the horizon for shadows, knowing that any day they were coming to swallow a land and a friend down into a maelstrom of red and shade?

And then there was her. Lilias. Still full of life. She didn't know it. He'd realized that tonight. She had no idea what bubbled inside of her. Questions haunted her eyes, and trouble had slowed her step. But the life hadn't burned out. It was still there.

He didn't have the answers. But he knew one thing—

My days are about to become—

Very interesting.

AFTERWORD

- Desmond and Lilias' story will continue in the SPECTRUM DUOLOGY. For updates, follow Bryn on Instagram (brshutt) and signup for her newsletter at brynshutt.com

THANK YOU

Thank you, dear reader, for diving into my world of mercenaries, monsters, and madness. I know there are so many stories out there, and I am honored that you took a chance with mine.

A special thanks to Hannah W and Micheline. You ladies are my emotional support humans. Hannah, *Illuminare* has all your boys (well, most of them). And Micheline, now we can finally finish our Sleeping Beauty story!

Thank you to my cover artist, Julia, and to my illustrators: Irina, Kateryna, and Hannah R. All of you are so talented and amazing and deserve the best!

To Ireen for the Laude, Kennet, and Des art. Kennet wishes the story happened that way. I love it.

To Marcella for the Luca portrait. It's exquisite.

A shout-out to my editor, Deborah. My stories would be madness without you.

To all my early readers—thank you for all your input, cheers, head shakes, and for giving me the push to get this file off my computer and free out into the world.

To Anastasis for being there.

Thank you, Mary, for all the violin expertise and advice!

To my writing groups on Slack and Facebook—thank you for every answer to every random (weird or otherwise) question and for all your encouragement.

Dearest family—no, Mum, this isn't "that story." Not yet, but some day. But it is a book. I finally got to grow up and be like you. Stephen, for all the graphics and our shared love of fantasy—even if we're still arguing over which book Tim Gerard Reynolds narrates the best.

And lastly and most importantly, to my Lord and Saviour Jesus Christ, the one who conquered death and ever lives to make intercession to those who come unto God by him.

About the Author

Bryn Shutt is a bookseller by day, fantasy writer by night, and Kdrama addict in between. She lives with her husband and animal kingdom in the Blue Ridge Mountains.

ONE LAST THING

Thank you for reading! Reviews help authors and potential readers so much. So, if you enjoyed this story (or were just happy there was punctuation), please consider leaving a review on Amazon or Goodreads. You will have my eternal gratitude (which is a very intangible thing, but know that it's real).

bryn

www.ingramcontent.com/pod-product-compliance
Lightning Source LLC
Chambersburg PA
CBHW020336310726
48979CB00015B/2390/J
* 9 7 8 0 9 9 1 5 8 3 3 5 5 *